Saving Scarlett

RANDA GOODE

Copyright © 2013 Randa Goode

Trail Media
1320 Ynez Place 181306
Coronado, CA 92178
ChisholmTrailMedia.com
Facebook.com/TrailMediaLLC
Twitter: @TrailMediaLLC

All rights reserved. No part of this publication may be reproduced, distributed, or transmitted in any form or by any means, including photocopying, recording, or other electronic or mechanical methods, without the prior written permission of the publisher, except in the case of brief quotations embodied in critical reviews and certain other noncommercial uses permitted by copyright law. For permission requests, write to the publisher, addressed "Attention: Permissions Coordinator," at the above address.

Printed in the United States of America
ISBN-13: 978-1492806394 (Trail Media)
ISBN-10: 1492806390

Cover and interior layout designed by: Freestar Design Group

For Mia, Shadi, and Natasha
Thanks for everything

Acknowledgement

Writing a book is not a lone project, and because of that, I would like to thank the following:

Thank you Melanie for introducing me to Dana. None of this would be possible without that.

Thank you Mia, Shadi, and Natasha for carrying on endless conversations about imaginary people and not locking me away because of it. Sorry, Natasha, that I couldn't get the names just right.

Thank you to all my co-workers and friends who have come along with me on this journey, sharing in my excitement.

Thank you Dana and Christina for loving the story as much as I do and taking a chance on me even before Scarlett was Scarlett.

And last, but certainty not least, thank you to my husband and kids, to my mom and dad, my sister and brother, and all my nieces and nephews. I know it's hard on you when I transport to the world in my head. But thank you for always putting up with me, believing in me, and cheering me on when I wasn't sure if I could do it.

I love you all.

Saving Scarlett

HELL IS EMPTY
ALL THE DEVILS ARE HERE
~William Shakespear

Chapter One

I crammed twenty-eight dollars of tip money into the glass jar sitting on my dresser just as the thud from a car door sounded in the driveway. Mom was home.

My chest felt suddenly heavy as I thought about her stumbling down the hallway, holding the walls for support, knocking the few pictures that still remained to the ground, only to tell me about another one of her reckless nights. I flicked the light off and hurried beneath the covers, still wearing my jeans and a red Luigi's Pizza T-shirt that reeked of garlic, and settled in just before my bedroom door creaked open.

Breathless and silent, I waited for her to register that I was asleep before she headed to do the same thing. But the door remained open for too long and an eerie silence settled in the room.

What was she doing?

Then all at once, panic set in when a heavy footstep fell against the hardwood floor - a footstep that wasn't Mom's. Shifting, I saw the silhouette of a man, greasy and overweight, standing at my dresser. But even from the dim light from the hallway, I knew who it was - Frank Bradford

– Mom's somewhat boyfriend.

To me, he was the human equivalent of a cockroach, scurrying around the house, eating what he could, taking what wasn't his, until someone clicked on the light to expose his laziness and lies. Then Frank would move on to the next house, to the next woman.

And it wasn't like Mom didn't know what kind of man Frank was. She had heard all the rumors. It was only a couple of weeks ago when she caught him at Sheila Stephenson's house in nothing but his boxer shorts and an apologetic grin.

Still, Frank knew all he had to do was give Mom a few days to cool off, then beg for her forgiveness. She bought it every time.

"What are you doing?" I demanded as I clicked on the lamp near my bed.

Frank spun around, his sausage fingers fumbling around in the glass jar. "I thought you were asleep," he grumbled.

"Yeah, I figured that."

His dark eyes, bloodshot and glassy, narrowed as I flung off the covers, crossed the room in two hurried steps and grabbed for the jar. "Give it back!"

"No," Frank said as he splayed his free hand, warm and sweaty, across my face and shoved me into the bookshelf, knocking me to the ground and sending books raining down on top of me.

Before I could get to my feet, Frank emptied the jar on my bed and scooped up all he could in a single swipe before hobbling out the door.

I leapt up and hurried after him, slipping on the books, bouncing off the door jam, before finally hitching his arm. "Stop," I said.

His elbow smashed against my face, sending pain through my nose milliseconds before the blood.

"Look what you did," I screamed, fighting back tears as my hand turned red.

But Frank didn't care. He just kept walking into the living room, shoving my money into his pocket as if nothing happened. I followed him.

"What's going on?" Mom said, getting up from the couch.

"He stole my money!"

Frank scoffed. "Why would I do that?"

"Because *you* don't have a job."

Hate blazed in his eyes. "I didn't steal your money," he said.

"Yes, you did!"

Frank turned to Mom. "Are you going to just let her talk to me like that?"

Mom's resolve wilted under Frank's glare and the effects of alcohol. Her brow crinkled as she turned to me. "Now, Scarlett," she slurred, "you can't just go around accusing people of things."

"I saw him do it, Mom."

She stood there for a minute, unsure, before Frank snuggled up to her and whispered in her ear. "Are you going to believe a kid over me?"

"I'm eighteen," I said. "Old enough for the police to take me seriously."

A white flash sent me to the floor and the unmistakable taste of iron filled my mouth. When the room came back into existence, Frank stood over me, his hand smeared with my blood. "I said I didn't take it!"

Mom stood behind him, her arms folded in defeat. She wasn't going to do anything. Not now. Not ever.

Standing, the world felt uneven beneath me as I let the blood splat to the floor in perfect circles. "I don't need this," I said, hating the way the quiver in my voice betrayed me. "I don't need any of it."

I stumbled back to my room and locked myself inside.

A few moments later, Mom knocked softly on the door. "Scarlett," she said, her voice as frail as her determination to protect me.

But she was too late. I was already digging out two bags from my closet and shoving in as many clothes as I could fit into them.

"C'mon, Scarlett," she said again.

And again, I refused to listen to her as I reached beneath my bed and pulled out a shoebox marked COLLEGE, then shoved the rubber-banded stacks of tip money into my purse. I got to my feet, grabbed the vintage camera Mom had given me two Christmases back and the dreamcatcher my sister, Hazel, had made me a long time ago, and added them to my haul. I stepped back and looked around to see if I had missed anything.

I should just leave the rest of it, I thought to myself, looking at the mess of books beneath the shelf, the uneven bed, the shabby curtains that never kept the light out. I wouldn't miss any of it. Not really.

And in a single breath, the room morphed into something unrecognizable. A place that no longer belonged to me. A place that was no longer home.

When I unlocked the door, Mom fell into the room and onto the bed, struggling to regain her balance as I scooted into the hallway and then into the living room. Frank sat on the couch, his boots propped on the rickety coffee table, his eyes fixed on the television, and my money still in his pocket.

As I tore open the front door, I had always imagined what leaving home would feel like, and in every scenario, I imagined myself sadder. I imagined myself hesitating. But now I was bursting free from the house and into the summer night, running to my car.

Through the passenger's side window, I watched Mom walk past the open front door just as I brought the engine to life. A part of me wanted to go back inside and make her come away with me and leave all this behind. But I knew if I went back, all that was waiting was lifetime of regret, a lifetime of wishing I had left when I had the chance. As I pulled from the curb, a knot lodged itself in my throat.

I couldn't save her.

I could barely save myself.

***

The road sign for Lost Creek gleamed in the headlights and I took the exit, feeling a rush of fear bubble up inside me. But this sudden panic wasn't from the town, but at the thought of seeing Hazel again.

I wasn't even sure why I came here. Maybe because I had nowhere else to go. Maybe because it had been three years since I'd seen Hazel and I missed her. But whatever the reason, a small part of me wished I had just stayed on the highway.

I mean, what if Hazel didn't want to see me? What if she didn't want to be found? It wasn't like she had sent me an invitation to come visit. All I'd ever gotten from her since she left was a graduation card two weeks ago. I glanced over at the envelope sticking out of my bag, the edges already worn from the many nights I laid on my bed, staring at Hazel's handwriting, all curly and bubbly. I wondered how she selected the card or if she struggled with the inscription, testing out several, before deciding on "Best of luck" because she couldn't think of anything else to write. It wasn't really the come-and-see-me-when-you're-in-town kind of offer that I was making it out to be. But even so, Hazel was my sister, and if anyone would understand why I was running, it would be her.

A yellow warning light flashed about a mile down the road, breaking up the stillness of the early morning. Beyond that was Lost Creek, a small town nestled among tall pines. The sun had yet to break from the earth, but the darkness had started to brighten into a soft gray.

As I slowed the car, leaning forward on the steering wheel and stretching out my tight muscles, something broke through the shadows a few yards in front of my headlights, then paused on the road.

"What is that?" I said to myself, stopping the car.

A bear? A person?

I blinked into the darkness, straining to make out details, disbelieving my eyes when murky streams swirled from the mass in front of me like ribbons on the wind. Inching closer, I fought the voice in my head that screamed for me to just drive around it. But I couldn't just go. I wanted to know what it was.

Every movement I made, it countered, drifting back toward Lost Creek, keeping itself just beyond the headlights. I put the car in park and sat there as the thing floated from one side of the road to the other. After a long second, I swallowed back my fear and opened the car door. The cool morning air startled my senses, and for a moment, I assumed the creature would dart back into the forest, leaving me forever wondering what it was. Instead, it anchored itself on the concrete and stretched its long arms out by its side, like it was daring my advance.

The soft wind shifted around me, bringing with it a sense of dread, and this time, the voice in my head won out and I jumped back into my car, locking the doors. The creature grew from its midsection, expanding until I was leaning over my steering wheel to see the top of it.

My hand shook as I yanked the car into gear, grinding the transmission, then stomping on the gas. I squinted my eyes shut and braced myself against the inevitable crash, but after a few feet, I opened my eyes when I was still going.

I adjusted my rearview mirror, scanning the barren road, startled to see that it was clear.

Maybe I should get check for a concussion, I thought, willing myself to believe that I had imagined the whole thing. But I still found myself checking the rearview mirror a second time and pressing the gas pedal harder, just in case.

I pulled into the parking lot of The Spot, a little restaurant and shop nestled at the base of the bridge that stretched across Lost Creek Lake. Inside, every inch was filled with some kitschy memorabilia of past decades: lava lamps next to WWII pinup girls, surfboards as shelving for roller skates and a Superman lunchbox, Star Wars bobblehead dolls guarding the register, and framed record covers surrounding a jukebox with Patsy Cline crooning away about being crazy. The clientele looked like a mixture of families on vacation, all dressed shorts and T-shirts covering swimsuits for a day on the lake, with a few tables of fisherman getting in a bite before heading out.

In the back, two waitresses moved like worker bees from one table to the other, refilling coffee and delivering plates of warm breakfast. I sat down at the counter and unfolded the menu, pausing when everything fell quiet.

I glanced around and was surprised to see everyone was staring at me. What was the big deal? Had they never had a stranger in town? Had they...

Everything made sense when I caught my reflection in a chrome napkin dispenser. I pushed back from the counter and rushed to the restroom. In a frenzy, I washed away the dried blood smeared on my cheek and around my nose.

Everyone knew. Everyone saw.

Then the burn of crying rose in my throat as I studied the large bruise above my right eyebrow. And when I blinked, I turned to a blur in the mirror. I wasn't even me anymore.

"It will be better today," I told myself as I pushed out a long breath, then wiped my face dry. But when I checked the mirror again, I wasn't alone.

A girl, about my age with dark hair and dark eyes, stood behind me with an expression I couldn't read.

"You okay?" she asked as I stepped back to give her room at the single sink.

"Yeah," I said with a quick sniffle as I used the paper towel to make one last swipe across my face.

When she caught my attention again in the mirror, I pulled open my bag and rooted around long enough to find a cheap pair of sunglasses. I was relieved to see her lose interest and walk back into the restaurant.

The thud of the closing door echoed against the tile as I slipped on my glasses, then took another deep breath before leaving the sanctuary of the restroom. In the cafe, I could feel the stares again and hear the whispers. I wanted nothing more than for the floor to open up and swallow me whole. But since that didn't happen, I grabbed packaged donuts, a chocolate milk, and a *Find Yourself in Lost Creek* guidebook, then headed to the front, getting in line behind a man with a graying ponytail.

When it was my turn to checkout, I huffed when I saw that the clerk was the girl from the restroom. She studied me as she smacked on a piece of gum, tapping her blue fingernails on the laminate between us. I felt like she was about to grab the microphone next to her and announce my situation over the loudspeaker to anyone who may have missed my horrendous entrance a few minutes earlier.

Please don't say anything, I silently pleaded as I considered just leaving my breakfast and bolting out the door.

"So," she said slowly, fingernails still drumming on the counter, "you staying in town?"

I slowly realized she wasn't about to openly humiliate me, and my anticipation deflated like a leaky balloon. I blinked at her from behind the glasses, then followed her hand to the guide. "Thinking about it," I said as I pushed the cash across the counter and grabbed the chocolate milk.

"Cool," she said as she handed me back the change. "Welcome to Lost Creek."

Outside, I checked my phone and immediately tossed it back into my bag when I saw I didn't have a signal.

Of course, I thought as I worked at convincing myself that everything was fine. I tried to focus on the warmth of the morning sun on my skin and the humid air, already thick and hard to breathe. But then all the pressure of the last twelve hours careened back into my body when I noticed a red Jeep sitting directly behind my white Taurus, blocking me in.

Ducking beneath a pair of raggedy fishing poles poking out the back, I peeked inside for some clue about who it belonged to. All I could see were clumps of mud and wadded up clothes littering the passenger's side floorboard, while in the back were two large boxes next to one smaller box with "Fragile" stamped on the side, sitting with the poles angled against it.

You have got to be kidding me, I thought. I half expected that, at any minute, someone was going to come out of their hiding spot, laughing at the look on my face. But five minutes passed and there was no someone, there was no laughing. There was only me, standing in the heat with sweat dripping down my back.

I hoisted myself onto the step-bar and pressed the horn, letting it blare. It had a distinct sound, low and deep, that cut through the serenity of the morning. Drivers on the bridge stared, people pulling into the parking lot stopped, and a guy, about eighteen or nineteen, rushed out the door of The Spot.

Mud was splattered on his jeans, his shirt looked like he'd pull it from the bottom of his laundry basket, and a pair of dark shades hung from a necklace made of a long strip of leather tied around three silver rings. In spite of his haggard appearance, he was sort of gorgeous: over six feet tall with dark hair and olive skin. But when he grabbed my arm and yanked me down from the Jeep, all his appeal vanished.

"What's wrong with you?" he spat, his green eyes narrowing.

I motioned to my car. "I'm not the one blocking people in."

"I wasn't going to be in there very long."

"I've been out here for five minutes," I said, waving the Lost Creek brochure in his face. "How was I supposed to know how long you were gonna be? It wasn't like you left a note or anything."

He snatched the brochure from my hand and scoffed. "Should've figured."

"Figured what?" I asked, yanking the brochure back and tucking it in my pocket so he couldn't do that again.

"That you're a Townie."

"A what?"

"A Townie," he said slowly, like I couldn't understand English.

"Is that some stupid name you call visitors?"

He pushed out some kind of snort that was supposed to be a laugh but didn't answer.

"You're lucky," I said, stepping closer to him. "You're lucky I didn't just use my Townie car to ram this redneck-mobile out of the way!"

He blinked at me as the little muscles in his jaw flexed and then he drew in a breath of air like he was going to say something else. But, instead, he withdrew his sunglasses from his necklace, climbed into the Jeep, and peeled out onto the bridge.

What a jerk, I thought as I squinted after his departing Jeep.

After he was gone, I retrieved the brochure and spread it out on the hood of my car, smoothing out the folds to make it flat. I soon found my sister's street, Bear Paw Lane, and concluded that it was just over the bridge, about a mile away.

Tall pine trees stood guard on either side of the sun speckled the streets as I pulled onto Bear Paw Lane, creeping my car down the road. The shady lane was filled with grand homes on wooded lots with fancy flowerbeds and manicured lawns, the kind of neighborhood where people used their three-car garages to park their vehicles instead of as storage units. At the end of the road, I came to the home address on the envelope. Large paned windows lined the front of a yellow, two-story cottage that looked like it came out of a magazine, complete with brightly colored flowers and a cobblestone path that led around the side of the house and down to the dark waters of the lake.

I killed the engine and then sat in my car, watching the windows of the house, searching for some obvious sign that Hazel lived there. After a few scans of the property, I realized I had no idea what I was really looking for - other than a sign over the door that read: Hazel's House. But since none of the homes had anything like that, I climbed from the car.

With every step toward the door, my heart hammered against my chest and my palms sweat enough that I had to wipe them on my jeans. I centered myself with the grapevine wreath that hung from the door and took a deep breath before knocking. After a moment of silence, I heard someone stirring and then a man, brown haired and clean shaven, swung the door open.

"Can I help you?" he asked.

I stared at him for a long minute, taking in his khaki Bermuda shorts, navy polo, and brown boat shoes. "Does Hazel live here?" I finally choked out.

His brow creased and he seemed surprised by my question, like he was expecting me to be selling Girl Scout cookies or something. "Just a sec," he said, stepping back and calling for her.

It felt surreal, like I was still sitting back in my car, watching myself wait to see Hazel. Would she look the same? Would she think I did? Would she even recognize me? But when Hazel finally reached the door and pulled it open wider, every thought, every question left my head as I stared at her ginormous pregnant belly.

Chapter Two

"You're pregnant?" I said, like that was way more absurd than me just showing up on her doorstep unannounced after three years.

"And married," Hazel added without moving, other than quickly flashing her chunk of a ring. Still standing on the other side of the doorway, she motioned to the man who had answered the door. "This is Mark, my husband."

"Husband? Well...why...how?" I stumbled.

"What are doing here?" Hazel asked flatly.

Her question stopped my stammering and I lowered the sunglasses, giving her the answer without having to say a word. A part of me thought she'd be surprised, or at least a little shocked. But instead, she just pressed her lips together in a tight line, let out a long breath through her nose, and then said, "Come on in and I'll get you cleaned up."

The inside of the house matched the exterior - all light, cheerful, and perfect, with the faintest scent of vanilla in the air. As the door closed behind us, Mark shoved his hands into his pockets before awkwardly excusing himself to the study.

"You can use the upstairs bathroom," Hazel said, starting up the staircase.

I followed her up to the landing and down a short hallway, glancing at the pictures on the wall of Hazel's life with Mark. She seemed so happy. So different.

When we stopped at the door to a small dressing area just outside a bathroom and she clicked on the light, I couldn't help but stare at her belly. "When are you due?" I asked.

"Six weeks," Hazel said in that same flat tone as before, then motioned to the door on the other side of the small room. "There's some little travel shampoos and soaps in the basket by the tub."

"Thanks," I said as I scooted past her, catching a glimpse of us in the arched mirror. We were so different, Hazel and me. Her with her dark wavy hair and olive complexion like Mom, me with straight red hair and skin so pale you could practically see through it. But it was our brown eyes - our dad's eyes - that connected us. At least, in appearance.

Hazel's attention moved to my forehead and when I blinked it seemed as if the warm glow from the lights suddenly accentuated the bump on my brow and the dark circles beneath my eyes. I turned back to Hazel, and I wanted to tell her that it wasn't as bad as it looked, that I was okay. But when I opened my mouth, the words dried up and Hazel pulled the door shut.

After the shower, I wanted to feel better - to feel clean and whole again. But when I stepped from behind the beige curtain and wrapped myself in an oversized towel, tears spilled over without warning. It smelled so fresh, so clean and different that I couldn't help but feel far away from home. I sat there, crying, knowing it was stupid to feel so lost, so temporary, from the scent of fabric, but I couldn't stop myself. Maybe because I wasn't sure the emptiness inside me would ever go away. Maybe because I wasn't sure I would ever feel that I was home again.

It seemed like I had cried for an hour when the tears finally subsided. I washed my face with cold water, trying to undo the swelling beneath my eyes and forget the fears that screamed in my head. But I sighed when I looked in the mirror and realized that they both remained.

Heading downstairs, I stopped just before the descent when I saw the baby's room. I stepped inside, trying to slow my breath as it seemed to rage in the silence. A pink-and-white striped wall on the left side of the room stood guard over the crib that waited expectantly for the new arrival, with a changing table and rocking chair sitting opposite.

I stood there for a long minute, searching for some kind of optimism, some kind of hope, in this alternate world where I found myself. A world where Hazel, the girl who used to make my breakfast and braid my hair before school, the girl who used to help me with my homework and cook dinner when Mom was out on one of her dates, had somehow found a way to do what I was trying to do: build a new reality for herself.

But in the quietness, I realized the room looked just as foreign, just as strange, as my room had appeared last night. This was not *my* new reality. This was not *my* home.

Feeling the tears fighting to make a reappearance, I backed out of the room and headed downstairs, finding Hazel in the kitchen. I watched her for minute, stirring a pitcher of lemonade, looking strong and frail in the same breath. I wondered what Mom would have said if I had somehow convinced her to get into the car last night and we had come here together. Would she be crying right now, asking for a bottle of something to take the edge off? Or would she have the same, strange blister of anger I had that she was just now finding out about the baby... and Mark?

Hazel turned and caught me staring. "Have a seat," she said, motioning to the table like I was just someone who had stopped by for a chat.

The ice clinked and cracked as she handed me a glass of lemonade, then took a chair across from me. I watched the streams of condensation race down the sides while I worked to ignore the uneasy feeling growing in my gut.

Hazel took a drink, then looked out the window at the lake, her mind elsewhere.

"You have a nice house," I said in a voice louder than I intended.

"Thanks." She set her glass on the table. "Look, Scarlett," she said, then paused.

When I was three, a freak winter storm came through and froze Hawkins Lake. I don't remember all the details, just flashes of memory like lightening bus in the darkness. I remember Hazel and I following a group of older kids out on it, then the stinging cold when I fell through the ice, the silent water, the stranger pulling me out, the burning in my nose and throat.

But as I sat there, watching Hazel search for the right words, it felt like I was back beneath the surface, about to drown all over again. I pushed from the table and her impending speech, regretting every mile I drove to get here.

"Just save it, Hazel," I said, my voice quivering as much as my hands were now. "I didn't want anything. I don't even know why I came here." I swallowed back the lump that was threatening to suffocate me as Hazel stared. "I didn't come here to ruin your perfect life."

"Will you just sit down and quit being so dramatic?"

"For what? So you can feel better about telling me to leave?" I said, throwing my hands into the air for added affect. "I get it. I don't have to sit down to hear it."

"You think I want you to leave?" she said, her voice a whisper.

I blinked at her, uncertain of anything anymore.

"And send you where?" she asked. "Back to Mom's?"

Her words stung as hard as if she'd slapped me across the face, and without warning, a tear raced down my cheek. I wiped it away with the back of my hand. "Like I said, I didn't come here for anything."

"Yes, you did," she said. "You need a place to stay."

Again, her words were sharp, leaving me silent.

"We have the boathouse out there," she said, motioning toward the lake. "I've already talked to Mark and it's yours, if you want it. You know, just until you figure out what you want to do."

I stood there, wondering what the catch was, wondering why she would offer it to me. But even with all the doubts about her motivation circling me like a kettle of vultures, Hazel was right. I had come here for a place to stay. And we both knew it.

"I'll be out here by the fall," I said.

"And where will you go then?"

"To college," I snipped, excluding the part about still needing money for the dorm.

"That's good," Hazel said, chewing on the inside of her lip, and for a moment, I could have sworn I saw a ghost of a smile flickered on her face before it turned hard again. Maybe it was from the newfound knowledge that I would be gone and out of her life in less than ninety days. But whatever the reason, all I saw now was a stern expression. She took another sip of lemonade and pushed herself away from the table. "All right then," she said, straining to get to her feet. "I'll get some fresh sheets and we'll get you settled in."

I followed Hazel across the grassy lawn, toward the boathouse that looked like a miniature version of their home on top of a boat dock. The bright summer sun beat down on us and the weathered-wood stairs creaked beneath our feet as we ascended to the top level. Inside the cozy living quarters, Hazel opened the double windows by the door, letting the lake breeze sweep through the living room and carry away the thick, stale air from seasons of being closed up.

"There're a few pots and pans and cooking utensils," she said, pointing to the kitchenette, "and a flashlight and first-aid kit beneath the sink." She placed the sheets on the full-sized mattress in the bedroom just off the living room, then rubbed the key to the boathouse in her hand like she was debating on whether or not to add anything to her previous sentence. I figured she was about to set out ground rules or something like that, but after a long minute, she placed the key on the counter. "If you need anything else, just let me know."

I stood in the middle of the living room, listening to the stairs whine as Hazel headed back to the yellow house. A gust of wind burst through the front windows that overlooked the lake and billowed the sheer curtains to the ceiling, making them look like waves on the ocean. I turned my attention to the vast openness in front of me, and as the sunlight glinted off the water's surface, I wondered if this was how Hazel felt her first night away from home: scared and excited, miserable and hopeful. Inhaling the fresh air, I wandered into the bedroom and collapsed onto the unmade bed, watching the fan circle above me until, finally, sleep overpowered me and I closed my eyes on a very long day.

☙☙☙❧❧

My stomach growled, waking me, and it took me a moment to remember all that had happened and where I was. I lay there, taking in the bright white wall and nautical pictures I'd failed to notice yesterday. Beyond the front windows, a sailboat with a blue stripe on its sail drifted by, and I wondered if Mom was worried about me. But with every second that passed, my inner voice grew louder and louder, until it was screaming that Mom had probably forgotten all about what had happened.

I checked my phone. Still no service.

So maybe she had tried to call me, but couldn't reach me because I'm apparently in the middle of nowhere. I looked at my phone again, seriously doubting that scenario.

She had most likely woken up yesterday afternoon with jutting hair and a headache large enough to make her draw the curtains tight. She may have even stumbled to my room and, seeing the pile of books still on the floor, thought to herself that she would get on to me about picking them up the next time she saw me. I pictured her getting ready to go out with Frank, globbing on mascara that would eventually end up beneath her eyes, all the while thinking I was at work or at a friend's house. It would take her a while to realize that I was gone and never coming back.

But maybe it was better like this, for her to slowly grow accustomed to my absence. Maybe one day, far in the future, something would remind her that there used to be a red-haired girl that hung around the house. She might even wonder whatever happened to me, but it wouldn't be a sad thought. No. It would probably be one of those fuzzy memories, like trying to recall a person's name you met briefly two summers ago.

A knot tangled in my stomach and I wondered why I even cared how, or even when, Mom would miss me. I'd spent the last year meticulously planning my escape from that wretchedness I used to call home - doing what I could to ensure my admission into a college on the other side of the country, filling out endless scholarship applications that awarded most of what I needed. What I hadn't planned was the change in the timing of my departure, and subtracting the remaining weeks left me adjusting everything.

But now with a place to stay, I could focus on my major needs: food and a new job. I climbed from bed and scoured the pantry, finding a sleeve of stale crackers that I was almost certain had been there since last summer, and I choked them down. The sun flooded through the windows, making large rectangles on the wood floors, as I dug out a pair of denim shorts and a white T-shirt and slipped them on. While I stood there, pulling my hair into a loose bun on top of my head, then dabbing on concealer to cover my bruise, I realized that in my frenzy of flight, I had left half of what I needed in the small bathroom back at Mom's, including my toothbrush and toothpaste.

I pushed out a long, exhausted breath. *Today will be better*, I said to myself, not quite believing every word as I took out a breath mint from my purse and popped it in my mouth before grabbing my keys and heading into town.

Cars lined Main Street and people littered the sidewalks, spilling out of stores before disappearing into another, and the grocery store was no exception with a line of vehicles waiting to pull into the small parking lot. After a few minutes of sitting in my car and not advancing, I pulled onto a side road and parked in front of an abandoned warehouse with broken windows and a worn, painted sign.

As I climbed from my car, I noticed another building, two lots over, that looked like an old movie house, complete with a vintage cinema marquee running up the side of the wall. The foyer stretched out from the building with a few busted light bulbs stuck beneath a white billboard that displayed a forsaken R and E.

In the muggy afternoon air, I wondered what it was about old buildings that fascinated me. Maybe their appeal was that they served as tangible evidence that something someone once thought they wanted for their life, thought they needed, could change. Maybe it was because they proved it was possible for someone to end a way of life, leaving it behind to start a new one. But whatever the reason, their allure washed over me and I could see my old life crumbling away, the windows boarded up, the insides gutted as I turned toward Main Street, reminding myself that I needed to add deodorant to my list of supplies.

At the next corner, the driver of a black Yukon, a man with dark shades and a Cabela's cap, let me pass as he leaned over to the woman beside him in the passenger seat who held up an unfolded Lost Creek guidebook. When I made it across the street, the vehicle behind them honked.

I jerked toward the sound and a fire ignited in my gut when the jerk with the red Jeep blared his horn again. I wanted to scream something like "It sucks being blocked in," but before I could decide on the appropriate slogan for his misfortune, he yanked his vehicle into the opposing lane, let out another long honk, and then sped around the unmoving Yukon.

The man in the Cabela's cap threw his hand up at the commotion as I pushed into the grocery store and retrieved a cart, wondering why I found the guy in the red Jeep so intolerable. Usually I got the person's name and a few personal traits before diving into the deep end of detestation, but this loathing toward him just came naturally. It was like breathing. I mean, who did he think he was? The Mayor of Lost Creek? Keeper of the...of the... what was that word he'd called me yesterday?

The search for the exact insult yanked to a stop when I clipped the heel of guy standing in the produce section and sent apples spilling across the floor. "I'm so sorry," I said, abandoning my cart to check his injury. "I didn't see you there. I didn't mean-"

"It's okay. I'm fine," he said reassuringly as he grabbed two apples at his feet.

I scurried to collect three more that had rolled over to the tomato display, then returned, reaching across him to put the apples back in place. "Really," I said, turning around to apologize again. "I'm so sorry."

And on that last word, I could feel my mouth hang open as I stared up at him in all his captivating splendor: his blond hair that contrasted against his flawless light-toast skin, his broad shoulders and muscular arms that tested the fabric of his white T-shirt, and the dark fringe of lashes that fenced in his steel blue eyes.

I knew I should have said something intelligent, even mumbling would have been better than just standing there, staring. But as he towered over me, his hand brushing slightly over mine as he rearranged the fruit, I was mesmerized.

"Is your cart okay?" he teased, knocking me from the

trance and bringing me back to the horrific mess I'd made.

"I really didn't mean to run over you," I said as my face flushed a thousand shades of red.

Then he smiled a simple, uncomplicated grin I couldn't help but return. "Really," he said, touching my shoulder and making me feel like I could melt right there. "It's okay. I'll survive." As he dropped his hand from my shoulder, he gave a quick wave. "Take it easy."

I had always heard of love at first sight, that feeling like you'd met you soul mate. And to set the record straight, this was definitely not that. But a strange sensation engulfed me, like he and I were somehow tethered together by some unseen force, and every step he took toward the front of the store, threatened to break that connection. Was I supposed to go after him? Get his name? Make sure he was really all right?

But when he stood in line behind a group of young girls and they turned toward him, all dreamy-eyed and giggly, I felt like a fool. There was no connection. No tether.

He was just a really hot guy.

That was what I was feeling.

◦◦◦◦

The air was cool as purple clouds from an unexpected summer storm filled the sky. I hurried to my car, slipping past people on the crowded sidewalk, hating myself for halfway searching for Mr. Take-It-Easy, who left the store without giving me so much as a second thought.

At the corner, a rush of wind and the smell of rain met me. I pushed on to my car, struggling against the gales, as the movie theatre stood across the street, brightly lit against the dark skies. As I deposited the bags, I spotted my camera in the backseat.

There were still a few moments before the storm reached Lost Creek, so I hurried to the theatre, pressing my back against the wall across the street to fit the entire structure in the viewfinder, then took the shot. After that, I positioned myself beneath the grand foyer so I could get the cinema sign with a few fragmented bulbs.

As I wound the film, the scent of the shower grew stronger. But from the look of the clouds, the storm was still a few minutes away. I rushed to the side of the building, finding nothing photo-worthy, so I pushed through an opening in a chain-linked fence to reach the back of the building. The alleyway was full of discarded boxes and busted beer bottles and a few raggedy weeds rising up against the concrete wall. But what interested me the most was the open door.

The air dimmed as rain blurred on the horizon. I glanced at the door again, wondering what the inside looked like, but as I took a step toward the building, a fat raindrop landed on my neck.

I squinted against the rain as it dropped around me, then climbed back through the fence and dashed to my car, sliding to a stop in the loose gravel when a patrol car sat next to mine.

The sheriff, a tall, slender man, peered in my side window.

"Is there a problem?" I asked, crossing the street.

When he abandoned his visual search of my car and turned, I could see he had a graying mustache that hid his lips. "No problem," he said, adjusting his utility belt. "Just trying to figure out who this car belonged to."

"Don't you just call in the license plates or something?" I asked, pulling my keys from my pocket.

He ignored my question and asked his own, "What were you doing over there?"

"Taking pictures," I said and held up the camera, suddenly feeling the need to supply proof.

His mustache twitched with what I thought was a grin. "Is that a film camera?"

"Yeah," I said, feeling stupid when I held it up again. "It's a lomography camera."

His eyes thinned into little slits. "I don't know about all that," he said slowly.

"It just does different things with the light, so the pictures are just more...distinct."

"Distinct, huh?"

I nodded, then squinted up at the sky again as a series of bigger rain drops hit the hoods of the cars, warning us of more to come.

"So, you just passing through Lost Creek?"

"No," I said, wondering if I should call a lawyer or something. "I'm staying with my sister, Hazel Young. I mean, Johnson."

"Over off Bear Paw Lane?"

I nodded again.

"Nice couple," he said. "And that baby should be

here soon, huh?"

I forced a smile to hid the grief that even the local sheriff had known about the baby before I had.

"So," he said, still ignoring the splatter of rain around us, "did you come to help with the baby?"

"No. I mean, yes, I'll help if she needs me to. But, I'm just here to get a job until the fall."

"You found one yet?"

I shook my head, jingling my keys, hoping he would get the hint that I wanted to get out of the rain. He didn't.

"Well, go on down to The Spot and ask for Jenny. They're always looking for help."

"Thanks," I said and unlocked my car.

Just before I pulled my door shut, he said, "Tell her Sheriff Reed sent you."

Through the window, I smiled at him with a thin grin, then started my engine and pulled away as the rain let loose, drenching Sheriff Reed as he watched me go.

Chapter Three

The Spot was the last place I wanted to go. I was almost certain they would have a picture of me on a bulletin board or something as the girl who caused a scene. But still, I needed a job, and a place that was *always* hiring was the best place to start.

Inside, Elvis Presley's "Jailhouse Rock" mixed with the hum of the storm. The same clerk I'd met yesterday stood behind the counter, straightening a shelf of Troll Dolls just above her head. I cleared my throat, hoping she wouldn't recognize me. No such luck.

"Look who it is," she said.

I forced a smile. "Is the owner here?"

"You're looking at her."

For a moment, I expected her to tell me she was just joking. But when she raised her eyebrows, waiting for me to continue, I realized she was serious. "Wait. You're Jenny? But you're only, what, eighteen, nineteen?" I sputtered.

"Yeah, what's that got to do with anything?"

"Nothing," I said, fumbling. "I just...how did you get all this?"

"From my dad," she said flatly. "Did you come here to ask about me, or...?"

"No, Sheriff Reed said you were hiring."

"Maybe," she said with the same unreadable expression she'd given me yesterday at the sink. "Have you decided if you're staying in Lost Creek yet?"

"Yeah," I said. "I'll be here until the fall."

Jenny reached next to the cash register, pulled out a clipboard with an application, and then slid me a pen. "Fill this out and bring it back to me."

I found a folding chair near a table displaying rain ponchos and scribbled out my information. As I was finishing up, the door opened and the owner of the red Jeep stomped inside. He slammed his hand on the counter, startling me, but barely jolting Jenny.

"What do you want, Riley?" Jenny said as evenly as if he was asking for a pack of gum.

"I want you to quit telling every Townie about *my* fishing hole."

Townie. That was what he called me.

"It's not just *your* fishing hole," she said. "The last time I checked that was federal land."

Riley ran his hand through his dark hair, making it a damp and towering mess on top of his head. "Jenny, you know it's dangerous out in those woods."

Huffing, Jenny slapped down a black bottle with a bright orange label. "That's why we sell bear repellant," she said, her eyes hard on Riley's face.

"We both know that stuff works about as well as throwing a pine cone. Just have those Townies fish under the bridge like everyone else."

Jenny crossed her arms and jutted her jaw. "I'll do no such thing. If those Townies you despise so much want to buy some extra lures and bear repellant for a chance to catch some stupid fish, then I'll draw 'em a map to Black Bear Falls if they want me to."

Pressing his hands on the counter, Riley leaned toward Jenny. "You don't understand," he said.

"I understand just fine, Riley," Jenny countered. "You want to keep your spot a secret, but that's just not gonna happen. You either need to learn how to share or find another hole."

Riley snarled as he backed away. "If one of them gets hurt, it's all on you," he said, pointing a hard finger in her face.

"Whatever."

Rage burned in his gaze when he spun around to leave and caught me eavesdropping. I wasn't sure if it was from the mutual dislike we held toward each other, from his conversation with Jenny, or a combination of the two. For a moment, I braced myself, anticipating Riley unleashing some of his frustration on me.

But then everything seemed to shift when the man with the graying ponytail from yesterday came barging in the door and grabbed Riley's shoulders.

"Where's the sheriff?" the man asked in between breaths.

Riley blinked at him and shrugged off his grip. "What's wrong, Bill?"

"I've seen something."

Jenny rolled her eyes and went back to straightening the shelf, but Riley's expression turned wary.

"What do you mean, you've seen something?"

Bill rubbed the back of his neck as his eyes darted from one side to the other. "I don't know," he said, his voice rickety. "I just don't know."

I found myself sitting on the edge of the folding chair, leaning to hear their conversation better, wondering if Bill had seen what I'd seen on the road yesterday. But before Bill said anything else, Riley opened the door. "Let's talk outside," he said, glaring at me as he followed Bill through the door.

I watched out the front window as Riley walked Bill back to his crookedly parked blue pickup, then opened the door. Bill kept shaking his head, trying to get a word in, but Riley repeatedly pointed to some unknown place in the universe, while at the same time, urged Bill to get into this truck. At first, I thought Riley was telling Bill where he could find the sheriff, but when Bill raised his head and stared at Riley for a long minute, with all the fire from his urgency gone, I had a feeling directions were not discussed.

Slowly, Bill climbed into his truck and started the engine. Riley hurried to his Jeep, following Bill from the parking lot, and they disappeared over the bridge.

"Who was that?" I asked, sliding the clipboard back to Jenny.

"Which one? Riley Shelton or Bill Dickerson?"

"Both of them."

Jenny sneered. "Well, Riley's just some local under

the delusion that just because his family has connections in this town, he has *certain* right over everyone else, if you know what I mean."

Kind of what I'd thought.

"And Bill's just some old kook with crazy stories about the woods."

"Is there any truth in his stories?" I asked, trying not to sound as crazy as Bill.

Jenny laughed. "Just depends on who you ask, I guess."

"Well, what has he seen?"

Jenny shrugged. "The boogyman, Big Foot," she huffed. "I don't know." She pulled the application from the clipboard. "Now, did you want to talk about Bill Dickerson or about a job?"

"A job."

"I see you've waitressed before," she said, nodding as she scanned the page. When she reached the bottom, she put the application to the side. "All right, here's the deal. If you work hard, we won't have a problem."

"Understood."

"You don't have a boyfriend, do you?"

"No."

"Good," she said. "We've had a few girls that found working Friday and Saturday nights at our Movies in the Moonlight interfered with their love life. This won't be a problem for you, will it?"

"No, I just got to town so..."

"All right," she said, sliding me a bright yellow shirt with a black dot in the middle.

"That's it?" I asked, taking the shirt. "I got the job?"

"Yep. See you tomorrow."

ಚಿಚಿಖಿಖಿ

The rain had settled into a drizzle, coating everything in a fine mist, when I parked in front of the yellow house. I unloaded my bags and camera from the backseat, then grabbed the dreamcatcher that was still on the floorboard before hurrying down the cobblestone path to the boathouse.

I had just reached the backyard when someone called my name.

"You get settled in okay?" Mark asked from a chair on the back porch, glancing at the bags in my hands, then getting to his feet. "Here, let me help you."

"No," I said, "I'm good."

But in less time than I expected, Mark was already in front of me, pulling the bags from my grip. He peeked inside the heaviest one, spotting six cans of Chicken Noodle soup. "Feeling a bit sick?"

"No, just not a great cook," I clarified.

"Ah," Mark said, "soup's a great cure for that, too."

A small grin jumped to my lips, but I quickly squashed it before Mark saw.

"We're grilling out later after the rain stops," he said to me over his shoulder as he climbed the stairs. "You can join us. That is, if you'd like something other than soup for dinner."

"No, I'm okay."

"It's really not that big of a deal, Scarlett. And besides," he said, stepping to the side so I could unlock the door, "I'm sure Hazel would love to catch up with you."

I laughed to myself as I shoved the key into the lock, fighting the urge to tell Mark he needed to get to know his wife a little bit better. The Hazel *I* knew left years ago and never gave me a second thought, much less wanted to catch up on what life was like with Mom. But maybe he was just naive and didn't understand that somehow, in our genetic makeup, we were able to cut all connections from one another and walk away without a single regret.

"What's that?" Mark asked, motioning to my arm.

"Oh," I said, "it's a dreamcatcher."

"I've don't think I've ever seen one quite like that before," he said as he set the bags on the kitchen counter.

I pulled it from beneath my arm so he could see it better. "It's really just an old Christmas wreath," I said. "Hazel made it for me a long time ago and she called it a dreamcatcher, so..."

"The name kinda stuck?"

"Yeah," I said.

He took it from me, inspecting the different trinkets hot-glued to the green fibers: a few pink Legos; a bright green, rubber dragonfly; an orange ribbon from one of Mom's shirts; a small, silver cross my sister had gotten for Easter one year; a Hello Kitty head; and a bow made from a striped tie Dad had once owned.

"I know it's ugly," I said, suddenly feeling self-conscious about it when Mark studied it too closely. "I don't even know why I brought it with me, really."

Mark handed it back. "I have this old blanket from when I was little and it has that same sentimental value," he said, noting the dreamcatcher. "But Hazel doesn't see it that way and wants me to just get rid of the old thing. I keep teasing her that if she's not nicer about it, we'll bring Anna home in it."

Every emotion balled up in my stomach at once. "The baby's name is Anna?" I asked, feeling like I'd just learned I had an extra finger or something.

"Anna Grace," Mark said, smiling. "My mom's pretty excited that we named her after my grandmother."

As Mark shifted back to his story about the blanket, the simple fact that the baby had a name - a family name - along with a whole group of people just waiting to meet her, gnawed at me. Maybe it wasn't Mark that needed to get to know Hazel better. Maybe it was me. Maybe this kind of family connection was what Hazel wanted in her new life - and she found it in Lost Creek with Mark. But if she had wanted family bonds, why did she search it out with complete strangers? Why didn't she just keep what she had with us?

Even with all the speculations and questions tumbling through my head, I still couldn't get over the way Mark easily revealed information about Anna, like he wasn't worried the slightest bit I may call Mom and tell her everything. Then the weight of realization draped over me. "Does my mom know?" I blurted, surprising myself with the sudden question.

"About the blanket?" Mark asked as his face

scrunched with confusion.

"No, about the baby? About Anna?"

I don't know what I was expecting. Maybe for him to tell me that, of course, she didn't know. That Hazel refused to share that kind news with her family because, well, we were who were. That maybe, for the sake of the baby, I should keep the information to myself and keep Mom unaware of Anna's existence and her new title as a grandmother. But what I wasn't expecting was for Mark to look me in the face and inform me that Mom had known all along.

A bubble of disbelief embedded itself in the top of my throat and I did my best to choke it back as I stared at Mark, waiting for him to tell me that he was just making some horrible joke. That Mom really didn't know anything about Hazel or her life. That Mom had been cut off from all communications, just like I had. But when he turned toward the door, I knew what he'd said was true.

"Well, I'll put an extra piece of chicken on," Mark said, unaware of my stupefied state, "in case you change your mind."

When Mark closed the door, I dropped into the chair by the table, listening to the stairs creak as he headed back to the yellow house, and understanding for the first time that Hazel hadn't cut *us* from her life. Just me.

The storm had passed and the aroma of grilled chicken seeped through every crack in the boathouse, making my stomach grumble with hunger even after I ate a bowl of soup. But I refused to join them for dinner. I mean, how could I? How could I look at Hazel now that I had proof she wanted nothing to do with me?

With a few more hours of daylight left, I slipped on a pair of flip-flops, grabbed my camera and headed out. When I reached the bottom of the staircase, Mark saw me and gave an enthusiastic wave, but then all his eagerness vanished when I turned toward the shoreline and kept walking.

Cutting through the neighbor's property that separated the yellow house from the forest, I gazed up at the massive log home, its back wall transparent with windows. I imagined the spectacular view they had from every spot in the house. The beautiful sunsets. The starry nights. But even with all the openness and grandeur, there was something empty about it.

I stepped from the St. Augustine grass and onto the sandy terrain that surrounded the lake. My feet sank easily into the soft earth as I ventured around the first bend, leaving suburbia behind. After a few yards, I found a large boulder, pulled out the Lost Creek brochure I had tucked in my back pocket and spread it across the rock. It took me a minute to find my location on the map, but after that, I moved my finger along the curve of the lake, noting that the trailhead for Black Bear Falls was around the next bend of the shore.

As I tucked the map back into my pocket, the conversation between Riley and Jenny screamed in my head. Was it actually dangerous out there? Had Bill really seen something too? Or had Jenny been right that Riley just wanted to keep his fishing hole to himself? Unsure if any of it was true, I collected a few rocks and tucked them into my front pocket just before spotting the wooden trail maker hidden in a clump of tall grass.

The path was smooth from wear and the sunlight cut through the lingering clouds, casting long lines of light through the trees, making the forest look safe and harmless. After another scan of my surroundings and finding nothing ominous, I stepped inside. Trail markers led me deeper into the woods, carrying me across downed trees and over small hills while birds chirped overhead.

The solitude of the forest was serene. I didn't have to worry about Mom or Hazel. I didn't have to worry about being cut out from people's lives. I didn't have to worry about anything other than breathing in the fresh air and making sure to step over an occasional exposed root.

Up ahead, another marker pointed to the left. I followed the curve of the path and the evenness of the trail vanished, replaced with jutting rocks and a sharp incline, making it a difficult climb in flip-flops. The hush of the falls grew louder as I wiggled between two large rocks, then I emerged at the peak of the cascade. The mist in the air clung to my skin, making it feel fresh and cool as I ventured to the edge to get a better look of the forest floor from that height.

The tall pines stretched out as far as I could see and birds flittered from one branch to another in the canopy.

I climbed down the other side of the peak, grabbing on to whatever I could find when my flip-flops slipped, and finally made my way to the pool of water beneath the falls. The air was much thicker and sultry down here, making me miss the chill from the mist at the top. But from this angle, I could see how the sunlight reflected from the constant ripple in the water and cast arches of light on the surrounding trees and rocks.

I moved a few more feet away from the falls and raised my camera, framing in the luminous trees and the white cascade from the waterfall, then snapped a shot. Two yards down, the pool narrowed into a stream small enough for me to cross. I hopped over and backed away from the falls, fitting the pool in my viewfinder, but as I shifted to level the shot, a movement at the peak caught my eye.

I lowered the camera and squinted up at the rocks, finding nothing. As I steadied the shot again, I paused once more when something dark raced between two rocks.

My heart lurched to my throat as I lowered the camera and dug the rocks from my front pocket, readying to hurl them. But as I scanned the rocky terrain for a second time, everything was still. Even the birds and insects seemed to have fallen silent.

Even though I couldn't see anything, the urge to run grew stronger the longer I stood there, staring at the falls. I yanked the map free from my back pocket and saw the blue line of the creek eventually merge into Lost Creek Lake, giving me an alternate route back to the yellow house. Dead limbs cracked beneath my feet as I hurried along the creek bed, glancing back after every few steps. After only a few minutes, I'd made it far enough away from the falls that when I looked back now, I couldn't see it anymore. But the feeling that I wasn't alone still haunted me.

The creek suddenly widened and then divided, leaving me stuck on the wrong side and pushing me deeper into the woods. I turned to go back to a narrower place to cross over again, but a crack echoed through the forest and I stopped. At first, I tried to tell myself that it was just a falling branch, but then it sounded again, this time closer. I pushed on as fast I as could, following the creek with saplings slapping me in the face, sharp sticks stabbing my feet, my breath sawing from my chest, until a wall of trees blocked my mangled path. Another crack of dead wood sounded from behind me as the hairs on the back of my neck and arms pricked out.

There's nothing there. There's nothing there, I said to myself. But the soft crunch of dried foliage told me I was wrong. The hard edge of the rock I still gripped in my hand pressed into my skin, and it took every ounce of strength I had to force myself to turn around.

It felt as if I was hovering above my body, watching myself struggle to confront whatever was following me. But when my eyes finally landed on the thing behind me, I was instantly squeezed back into my skin as I stared at the dark beast I'd seen yesterday on the road.

Chapter Four

Now in the fading light of the day, I could see this thing was real. Its contorted and mangled body bent and moved as it focused its yellow eyes on me. The claws on its three-toed feet pierced the sodden ground, collecting mud and pine needles each time it shifted from one leg to the other, while globs of black haze dripped from its lesioned skin like ink in water.

What was this thing?

Fear held me hostage as wafts of the dark mist slinked across the forest floor toward me. My heart banged against my chest as the fog grew closer, and when it brushed over my toes, the beating stopped completely and a coldness consumed me. Darkness closed in around my vision and my lungs burned with the craving for oxygen, begging me to breathe as I drowned in the moment.

I thought of the frozen lake, the stranger pulling me from the water and laying me on the ice, wiping the wet hair from my face.

I did not survive that to die here. Not like this.

With that thought, a fire ignited in my belly and a scream crawled from the depth of my soul and out of my mouth, piercing the deafening silence. I inhaled the sweet air, then hurled the rock I still clutched in my hand, hitting the beast in the head hard enough that it staggered back.

I turned toward the tree line and squeezed through a narrow opening between two pines. For a moment, I was stuck, wiggling like a worm on a hook as the monster regained its footing. I pulled in every inch of skin I had and pushed past the trees, falling into the soft branches of a juniper. The monster lurched forward. Its eager hand swiped at the open air, clenching and reaching in vain.

But in the next breath, the creature stopped and withdrew its arm. It stared at me through the small opening, the fire of hate flickering in its narrowed eyes as a deep grumble shook the earth. The monster jerked to the next opening, its hostility growing, and I staggered back, snagging my camera strap on a limb. I fumbled to free it and myself as the beast dug its claws into the bark, ripping it apart to get at me.

I knew I was going to die and no one would know why. No one was going to know what really happened.

Then all at once, I raised the camera and snapped a shot. If this thing was going to kill me, at least I would have a silent witness to my demise. But as I blinked away the brightness of the flash, I froze when I saw that the creature was gone and everything was quiet: no rustle of the leaves, no ripping of the bark, no growling of the monster.

I stood there, waiting for its sudden return, waiting for it to break through the tree barrier and sink its claws into my flesh and tear me apart. But after a few endless moments, the birds began to flutter overhead and the buzz of cicada returned to the forest. Somehow I knew, just like I did that early morning on my drive into town, that it was gone.

Disbelief and uncertainty pumped through me as I stared at the tall pines, thinking that whatever I had just seen could not really exist. But even as I stood there, I could see the deep gashes in the bark and the reality of the situation began to sink in. Hallucinations don't cause physical damage to trees or leave footprints on the ground. But what did I know? I woke up this morning thinking that monsters didn't exist.

I backed away from the wall of trees and pushed deeper into the brushwood, fighting to keep the spindly branches from cutting into my feet. After a short trek, I broke through the edge of the forest and stumbled out into the openness of the lakeshore.

But now, as the edge of the lake lapped against the shore, I thought about what just happened. It seemed fuzzy and distant, like a dream or something I'd seen in a movie. Yet even in the gathering twilight and the tranquil surroundings, I couldn't shake the anger I'd seen in the creature's eyes or the rage it had as it tore into the trees. Had Bill seen the same thing? Had this been what he wanted to tell the sheriff about earlier? Did Riley know too? If so, why was he trying to keep it from the sheriff? But before I could think any more about it, a crack sounded from the forest and I flinched into a full-out sprint.

My throat felt raw by the time the yellow house came into view. Strings of lights stretched across the back lawn, casting a warm glow to the fading day. Mark was still grilling like he had been, but now there was a crowd of others with him. I stopped at the edge of the neighbor's overgrown St. Augustine and leaned over, bracing my hands on my knees, trying to catch my breath as the murmur of conversation filtered through the evening air.

"You okay?" I heard someone ask.

I took two more deep inhales, then stopped breathing completely when Mr. Take-It-Easy from the grocery store sauntered over from the back of the log home. I just wanted him to keep walking or go back inside, to do whatever it was he was doing before he saw me, but the deep crease of worry on his forehead told me I wouldn't be that lucky.

My tongue was thick with thirst, but I gathered what little saliva I had left and coated my mouth. "I'm fine," I mumbled before returning to my impression of hyperventilation.

"Are you sure? You don't look fine."

And on his last word, everything swirled around me and my legs gave out, dropping me to the ground.

"Hey, hey, hey," he said, suddenly at my side and patting my back.

I tried to get to my feet again, feeling like a newborn fawn taking its first wobbly steps, but Mr. Take-It-Easy guided me back to the ground.

"Hold on, let's take it easy for a second," he said.

I was about to tell him that I was still fine, that this whole falling-to-pieces act was part of my everyday schedule. But when I turned my head and he leaned in closer, his breath rushing against my cheek as he draped his arm across my shoulder, speaking was no longer an option.

"C'mon now," he said, pulling me into his side. "It's gonna be okay. Trust me."

There was no logical reason to believe a single word he said. I mean, I didn't even know his real name. But there was something in the way he held me, shielding the horror from what I'd seen from seeping in too deep, and doing everything he could to keep me together long enough for the glue of self-preservation to take hold, that gave credit to his statement.

"What were you doing out there? What happened?" he asked softly in my ear as the setting sun glinted off the lake, illuminating his face.

I stared into his blue eyes, memorizing the small golden flakes around his pupil. But even with this newfound assurance I felt with him, I couldn't say the words. I couldn't blurt out a story like this and risk sounding crazy. Not in front of him. Not in front of anyone, for that matter. I wiggled from his arms and the terror that had lingered just out of reach now crashed back into me.

I couldn't figure out how he had turned off all the alarm and panic racing through me, like he'd flicked off a switch, with a simple touch. Was he some kind of saint? Some kind of answer to an unknown prayer?

"I was out for a jog," I lied, fighting back a wave of nausea, still wondering how his touch had kept all those emotions at bay.

Crossing his arms, Mr. Take-It-Easy leaned back on his heels as his face twisted in confusion. "In those?" he said as his gaze bounced from the camera to the flip-flops.

"Yeah," I said, sticking to my story.

He pushed out a long breath and got to his feet. "If you don't want to tell me, that's fine. But you don't have to lie to me."

"I wasn't lying," I said, lying again.

"Uh-huh."

"Scarlett," Mark called from next door, heading over with a pair tongs in his hand. "There you are."

"So you were just skipping out on the party, is that it?" Mr. Take-It-Easy asked me before Mark reached us.

"Sort of."

"So, I see you've met our neighbor, Blake," Mark said.

Blake looked down at me still on the ground, but remained silent. When I got to my feet and dusted the dirt off the back of my legs, Blake's annoyance from my blatant lie morphed into recognition. "You're the girl from the grocery store, aren't you?" he asked.

I could have lied about that too, but what was the point? He already knew. "Yeah."

I expected him to huff and walk away. And why not? I had already injured him, shown up on his back doorstep half-dead, and lied to him all in one day. But instead, a small grin pulled at the edges of his mouth. "Nice to meet you," he said, taking my hand and filling me with an overwhelming calmness.

"You want to join us? I just threw another round of chicken on the grill," Mark said to Blake.

As Blake dropped my hand, plunging me back into the sea of distress, it wasn't so much Mark's question that took me by surprise, but the overwhelming anticipation of Blake's answer and the utter disappointment I felt when he declined.

"Maybe next time," Mark said.

Blake's eyes held mine. "Maybe."

As I followed Mark over the property line, I glanced back at Blake, who was still standing there watching us go, and that tether stretched within me again. There was something in the way he stared that made me wonder if he felt it too. Maybe I should go back.

"Hungry?" Mark asked, breaking my connection with Blake.

"No, not really," I said as a tightness wrapped around my chest. People were everywhere, littering the back lawn, lounging on the patio. All unaware of what was lurking just beyond the tree line. And in the middle of them all, was Hazel, pregnant, laughing, and completely vulnerable. "What's Hazel doing out here?"

But Mark was the same as the others, oblivious. "Having fun, like everybody else," he said, handing me a paper plate with a piece of chicken. "This whole party was her idea."

"I'm not hungry," I said, handing the plate back to Mark.

"Are you sure?" Mark asked as he refused to reclaim it. "You should at least try it. I'm kind of known for being a genius at the grill."

"Fine," I said, pulling it back to me. "But, seriously, shouldn't Hazel be resting inside or something. I mean, in her condition and all?"

"What are you so worried about?" Mark asked. "Dr.

Shelton said she and the baby are doing fine."

I pushed out a long breath. "It's just... I heard something in town today," I said, pausing to find the right words. "Someone was saying they saw something, and..."

"Were you talking to Bill Dickerson?" Mark asked, laughing. "You know he's crazy, right?"

I sighed. "That's what I've heard."

Mark patted me on the shoulder. "There's no need to worry, Scarlett. There's nothing out there."

"You don't know that for sure," I said. "They discover new species in the rainforest every day. Who knows how many animals are out there that we don't know about."

Mark flipped a piece of chicken. "If I didn't know better, I'd say it sounds like you believe Bill's story."

"I didn't say that," I clarified. "All I was saying was that maybe outside in the open isn't the best place for Hazel."

Mark flashed a sideways grin as he went back to work at the grill. "So, you want to ask the hostess of the party to squirrel herself away for the rest of the evening because there's a chance that something from the rainforest may be lurking in the woods?"

"Well, no, I just...never mind."

"Tell you what," he said, halfway laughing as he flipped the pieces of chicken. "I'm appointing you as Hazel's personal bodyguard for the evening. Maybe you can protect her from the dangers lurking on the dessert table."

I knew he wasn't trying to be a jerk. He was just trying to get me to stay, hoping that maybe Hazel and I would strike up some conversation about the good ole' days and become the best of sisters again, but that just wasn't going to happen. I knew the truth now. I knew Hazel wanted nothing to do with me.

"You really should be more concerned," I said, "You're her husband."

"And you're her sister," he countered.

"Whatever." I yanked off a chunk of chicken and tossed it in my mouth, noting that Mark had been right about his whole genius-at-the-grill thing, but I wasn't about to admit it to him now.

"Besides," Mark said, smiling as he nodded to something behind me, "it looks like you have something else to be concerned about."

When I followed Mark's gaze, I was surprised to see Blake still there, his attention focused so intently on me that I stopped breathing for moment. "Does he always watch your parties like this?" I asked Mark.

"No," he said. "This is the longest I've seen him in one spot."

I didn't know what to say, but it was all I could do to force myself to look anywhere other than at Blake. After a long minute, I scooped some potato salad on my plate from bowl on a nearby table and headed toward an empty chair beneath a tall pine.

"Glad you enjoyed the chicken," Mark called out when I was a few feet away.

Mark probably thought I was just being absurd about the rumors in town. But he hadn't seen what I had seen. From across the lawn, Blake still kept his gaze on me, making it extremely awkward to chow down on a piece of chicken. And after every bite, I was still no closer to understanding how he'd done what he'd done.

But with everything that had happened today, I knew one of two things for certain: either I was as crazy as Bill Dickerson or there really was something out there.

I took another bite of chicken, wanting nothing more than for neither to be true.

Chapter Five

The sky was a dark blue with only a few fluffy clouds marring it. I slipped on a pair of shorts and a tank top and slid on my sunglasses. On the way out, I grabbed a worn paperback from the shelf near the couch and a beach blanket from the closet.

I couldn't help but look in the same area where I'd seen Blake last night, hoping to spot him again today. But all that was there were some trees and a few low bushes.

Sometime last night, between two of Mark's friends racing into the lake and the singing debut of a date of one of their neighbors, who mistakenly thought she sounded like Kelly Clarkson, Blake had slipped away into his log home. Before he had disappeared, I had thought that, after a while, he would venture over and join us. But instead, he kept his distance while keeping his focus on me.

A part of me felt it was kind of creepy-stalkerish, but another part felt safer with him around. How had he done that?

The grass was soft and cool against my bare feet as I found a spot near the shore, then spread out the blanket and settled in for a few minutes of sun before work.

It didn't take long for little beads of sweat to pool on my forehead as I skimmed the first chapter. The second chapter went by in a blur as I found myself wondering where Blake was instead of reading. And when I finished the third chapter and realized I didn't even know the main character's name, I shoved the book to the ground and huffed.

Where was he?

Yesterday, I had to just walk into the grocery store or cross his property line and he was there. But today, I was frying in the summer sun like a piece of fair-skinned bacon and he was nowhere to be found.

I started to gather my things, but then stopped when Hazel stepped out the back door in a royal blue maternity swimsuit and an oversized black sunhat. "Can I join you?" she called out as she waddled down the back steps.

"It's your house," I mumbled, opening up the book again.

Lowering herself to the blanket, her belly made it impossible for her to bend correctly, and the simple act ended up looking like a chore. When she finally made it to the ground, she leaned back to prop herself on her hands and stretched her face up to the sky. "This is nice," she said, exhaling.

Her statement stopped my make-believe reading and I wondered if she meant being out here with me or just out here in general. But when I stole a glance and saw her eyes closed in sun-soaked satisfaction, I remembered Mark's words and figured the latter.

I returned to the book, this time unable to concentrate because I kept thinking about Hazel. Why did she even bother coming out here? She had the entire day to do this, but waited until she thought I was trying to enjoy a few moments in the sun. Did she want to make sure she made life here as uncomfortable and awkward as possible, so I didn't get any ideas about staying longer than I needed to? If so, she didn't have to worry about that. I already had plans for my new life, just like she had three years ago.

"Be careful or you'll burn," she said, still facing the sky in all her olive-skinned glory.

The sting of overexposure was already scorching the back of my milky legs, but I stayed where I was and said, "I'm fine."

She shifted next to me and I could feel her focus had changed. "Mark told me you met Blake."

"Yeah," I said cautiously, sensing I was about to be bombarded with more cautionary comments.

But instead, she lowered herself to her elbows so she could see into my face. "He seems to like you."

"How do you know?" I said, my voice flat but my heart pounding.

She shrugged and her floppy hat wobbled on her head. "Everyone saw the way he was looking at you."

I had too. "So?"

"I'm just saying, he seemed...intrigued."

"Intrigued?"

"That's not a bad thing," Hazel said, rolling her eyes and turning back toward the sky.

I hadn't thought it was, but I let her statement linger in the air like I had, and I returned to my book.

After a few stressed filled minutes with neither of us saying a word, a jet-skier raced across the lake and whooped in excitement. Hazel took the break in silence as a sign to continue our forced conversation and added, "I just think Blake seems like your type."

I shoved the book to the blanket and pushed myself up to my knees, ignoring the sting in my skin. "*My type?*"

"You know, strong and athletic," she said, unaffected by my naked hostility.

"What do you know about my type? The last boyfriend you know about was Eric Reynolds from freshman year," I said, unable to stop the quiver in my voice. "And he wouldn't even know the difference between a baseball and a hockey puck."

"All I was saying was-"

"I know what you were saying," I choked out as a glob of emotion bubbled in my throat. "You were saying that you knew me. But you don't, remember? You left."

I grabbed the book and got to my feet. When Hazel looked up at me, she seemed so fragile. Maybe it was the roundness in her belly and her inability to move without difficulty. Or maybe it was from her lack of comment. But suddenly, I knew my words were harsher than I intended when I saw Hazel's eyes had glistened over. A part of me felt a twinge of guilt and wanted to pull the statement back, but the other part knew everything I had said was true and the tears in her eyes proved it.

"I've got to get ready for work," I said, leaving Hazel sitting there on the blanket and the wall between us as tall as ever.

Hazel was gone by the time I reemerged from the boathouse and that pang of guilt surged into full-on regret. I hadn't really thought anything I could say would matter to her. Why would it? She didn't want me here. She didn't even want me in her life. So why would she care what I thought?

I trudged across the grass and the emptiness of the back lawn matched the vacancy next door. Blake was still gone and the uncertainty of his location was enough to knock me from my remorse. I climbed in my car and checked for any activity next door, then tucked the disappointment in my pocket and drove to work.

The Beach Boys' *Good Vibrations* seeped out to the parking lot from The Spot and then met me full force when I stepped inside. Jenny glanced up and smiled from the register. "Hang on a sec," she called out to me and I moved to an empty place to the left of the door.

She stretched to the tips of toes to look over the sea of customers and waved toward the back, signaling a busty brunette who looked a few years older than me. The woman pushed to the front with her ponytail flipping from one side to the other and her bright, toothy grin in sync with passing glances.

The next customer in Jenny's line moved in place just as the woman from the back reached me, propping her hands on her hips. "You must be the new chick?" she called out over the music and the blend of conversation.

"That's me," I said. "But you can call me Scarlett."

"I'm Rachel," she said, then nodded toward the cafe. "C'mon."

It was like she was walking the red carpet, waving to her adoring fans, calling them by name, and I was her inconspicuous assistant trying to keep up and not fall on my face.

"It gets a little crazy in here," she said over her shoulder just before she turned on the charm again and waved at a woman and then her husband. "You ever waitress before?"

"At my last job."

I followed her behind the counter, but stopped when she bent down and rummaged through the lower cabinets. "Did you get fired or something?" she asked, pitching me a quick glance.

"No," I said, sounding more defensive than I meant to. "I moved."

She leaned back on her heels with an apron in her hand, then pushed back to standing. "Were you running away from something or to something?"

"What?" I asked as my mouth suddenly dried up.

"In my experience," Rachel said, handing me the apron, "people only move for those two reasons."

"I, uh…"

"You know what?" Rachel said, waving at my reply. "It doesn't matter. All I really care about is you doing your job." She reached across the bar and banged on the bell, summoning a thin, balding man. "This is Mel, our cook," Rachel said, then tilted her head like she was having trouble seeing the others through the narrow opening. "That's Marcus and the one in the far back is Mike, they're our busboys."

They gave an unenthusiastic wave and returned to scraping plates. "You place the orders and pick them up here," she said, motioning to the bar. "At the end of the night, ten percent of your tips go to the kitchen. That's non-negotiable."

"Fair enough."

I followed her from behind the counter, making mental notes on the locations of extra menus, wrapped silverware, straws, the drink station, and how to cash out customer's tickets. After we made the whirlwind tour of the inside, Rachel pushed out a side door and onto a deck that stretched from the building to the edge of the lake. Most of the weathered wood picnic tables were nestled at the edge of the railing, giving a great view of passing boats and the cluster of fisherman beneath the bridge, while a few of the other tables were scattered in the center.

"This half of the deck is your area," she said, gesturing to the left. "That half's mine and we don't share customers. That's non-negotiable either. Got it?"

"Got it."

Rachel reached into her apron and pulled out an order pad, tossing it to me along with a pen. "Any questions?"

I pushed the nervousness into the pit of my stomach, reminding myself I'd waited tables a thousand times and five different restaurants. I had this. "I'm good."

"All right," she said with an indulgent grin on her glossed lips. "The next customer's yours. After that, customer's choice."

I nodded, aware she had a clear advantage with the boardwalk entrance on her side of the deck, making it easier for her to get to customers first, but deep down, I knew I would have done the same thing if the roles were reversed.

It took a few minutes before the first set of footsteps sounded on the boardwalk. I was hoping for a twenty-something couple or a nice elderly pair to help ease me into my first shift. But instead, Sheriff Reed appeared with another man.

The sheriff was in his starched uniform and the other man in dark gray slacks and a white button-up shirt, both looking too formal, too dressy, to be eating on a deck. But they sauntered up the walk, waving at Rachel with the same familiarity as the other patrons inside.

"Sheriff Reed, Dr. Shelton," she sang, smiling brightly, then added a warning, "you're sitting with the new girl today."

Squashing the glare I felt building on my face, I stretched a warm smile instead and showed them to the table at the railing and furthest from the side door.

"I see you took my advice," Sheriff Reed said as he settled on the bench.

"Yeah, thanks for the tip," I said. "What can I get you to drink?"

"Just water for me," Sheriff Reed said.

Dr. Shelton added, "And two sweet teas."

"Is someone else joining you?" I asked.

Dr. Shelton leaned around me. "Ah, there he is."

I turned just in time to see Rachel practically swoon when Riley stepped onto the deck. "Hey, Riley," she said, her perfect smile falling. "If I'd known you were coming, I'd have set y'all in my section."

"Don't worry about it," he said, taking two steps and then stopping when he saw me. He spun back to Rachel. "What's *she* doing here?"

Rachel cupped her hand like she was whispering, but spoke loud enough that we could all hear her. "That's the new girl, Scarlett."

The muscles at the edges of Riley's jaw flexed as he looked back at me again. For a minute, I thought he was going to just turn around and walk away, but then Sheriff Reed said, "We're over here," like they were camouflaged in a crowd of diners and Riley was having trouble seeing them.

Riley's chest rose with a scornful sigh, then he closed the distance, his footsteps heavy and his movements rigid as he took the spot next to Dr. Shelton. Now that they were side-by-side, the man looked like an older version of Riley with the same dark hair, the same green eyes, the same dimple to the right of his mouth, and the same uncomfortable glare when they caught me staring. He was definitely his dad.

"I'll be back with the drinks," I said, hurrying from the table.

When Jenny had said Riley's family had connections, I had somehow pictured a shrewd family business or a large ranch that encompassed most of Lost Creek Lake, not that his dad was a doctor and they were friends with the sheriff. But I guess connections were connections.

When I returned, Rachel lingered in the open walkway next to Riley's table, talking to the sheriff. Across the table, Riley mindlessly scratched at the weathered wood with a pocket knife as the three silver rings at the end of his necklace swayed with his movement.

"You're gonna ruin that table," I said before I could stop myself.

Riley glared at me from beneath his brow, his green eyes hard, before returning to defacing the table.

"I asked you to stop," I said again flatly.

The ice clinked in the glasses as Rachel pushed a wide grin across her face, and then draped her arm around my shoulder, pulling me away from the table. "He isn't hurting anything," Rachel said in a syrupy voice.

"He's mutilating the table. How's that not hurting anything?"

"Look," she said, "I know we said we wouldn't switch, but what if I just take their table? You can take the next one."

"No," I said, fighting to keep the tray of drinks even. "They're in my section. No exceptions, remember?"

Rachel's grin morphed into a scowl. "Fine."

As she stomped to the other side of the deck, I returned to the table, setting the drinks out and trying to ignore Riley's blatant disregard to my request. When I pulled out straws and tossed them on the table, Riley jabbed the tip of his knife into the wood, leaving it standing on end while he unwrapped his straw. A smirk pulled at the edge of his mouth as he looked up at me, daring me to confront him again.

He's just a customer, he's just a tip. He's just a customer, he's just a tip, I reminded myself and pulled out my order pad. "Have you decided what you want?" I said, forcing myself to look anywhere other than at Riley.

"I'll take the Hit the Spot Sampler," Sheriff Reed said.

"I'll have the same," Dr. Shelton said, folding his menu.

"And you?" I asked, focusing hard on my handwriting as I waited for Riley to answer.

After a few silent seconds, I finally looked up, expecting him to be carving some crude picture of me in the table or snarling at me for breathing. But instead, his attention was focused on Bill Dickerson and another man who had just sat down in Rachel's section.

Unaware of Riley a few feet away, Bill sat with his back to the parking lot and nervously checked over his shoulder, pulling a Panama straw hat over his eyes in a fruitless attempt to disguise himself. He pressed his hands onto the table and leaned in toward the other man, and from the look on Bill's face, he was telling the horrid story Riley had fought to keep quiet.

But even with the truth spilling out of Bill like a punctured soda can, the other man just shook his head in doubt. Just like Mark had.

"I swear to you, Rob," Bill said, his voice rising with conviction. "I've never seen nothing like it."

I stood there, frozen. He *had* seen it.

"Bill, you sound crazy," Rob said.

"Well, what do you make of this?" Bill countered, pulling up the sleeve on his left arm and exposing a three-lined scratch.

There was a symmetry to it - an evenness that had to have come from claws. The same claws I'd seen rip into the bark of trees yesterday.

"What do you think you're doing?" Rachel asked as I suddenly found myself wandering closer to the men.

"I, I just..." I stuttered as I peeked around her to try to get a better look at Bill's arm.

But before I could explain myself to Rachel, Riley was already on his feet and at the table, gripping Bill's uninjured arm and pulling him from the table. "What'd I tell you, Bill?"

"This is a free country," Bill countered, fighting in vain to free himself. "I can say what I want."

"Not about this, you can't," Riley said through gritted teeth.

Sheriff Reed got to his feet and I wondered how Riley was going to keep this from him now that'd he'd seen it with his own eyes. But instead of asking questions, the sheriff just placed his hand on Riley's shoulder. "Now, let's all just take it easy."

Take it easy? Riley was openly threatening a citizen and all Sheriff Reed was going to say was take it easy?

Riley shrugged away from the sheriff and advanced on Bill again, gaining his attention. "You've already been told once," Riley growled.

"Like I said," Bill replied, straightening his shirt and regaining his composure. "It's a free country." He stepped from the table and started toward the exit with Rob following.

Sheriff Reed gripped Riley's arm, keeping him place like a dog on a leash. When Bill and Rob vanished around the building, Riley turned to Sheriff Reed. "Something's gotta be done about him."

Sheriff Reed's brow pulled down with worry. "I know."

"Then why are you just letting them walk away?" Riley asked, pointing a hard finger toward the empty boardwalk.

Sheriff Reed sighed. "Now's just not the time, Riley."

Chapter Six

Riley shrugged away from Sheriff Reed to go after Bill. At first, I thought Sheriff Reed would stop him again, but instead, he turned around and went back to his table like this was just another day in Lost Creek. Even Dr. Shelton just sat at the table, drinking sweet tea, unaffected by his son's behavior.

Jenny *had* been right about Riley thinking he had certain entitlements. And why not, especially when the sheriff was the one giving him advice on how to take care of the problem without leaving any witnesses?

Even his dad didn't seem to mind, as long as it didn't interfere with lunch. But even so, I wasn't a local and I wasn't under this fallacy that nothing could be done about it.

I turned to Sheriff Reed. "What was all that about?"

Sheriff Reed glanced up, squinting against the sun. "What do you mean?"

"All that," I said as I motioned to the empty table. "Does this have something to do with what Bill's been saying about something in the woods?"

His eyes narrowed even more, making them just

a sliver on his face. "Bill didn't say anything about the woods, Ms. Young. You got something you want to file a report about?"

Something inside me screamed that I was close to stepping over a line I wasn't sure I wanted to cross just yet. I swallowed back a lump that suddenly lodged itself in my throat and lied, "No." I dared a quick glance at Riley's dad, then wished I hadn't when he was staring at me just as hard. "I just heard –"

"I don't know what you *heard*, Ms. Young, but none of this is your concern. Do you understand?"

I blinked at Sheriff Reed, knowing I should just shut up about the whole thing and take their food order, but something in my gut wouldn't let me. "Not my concern? Didn't you see what happened to Bill's arm? If there's something out there hurting people, I think it's *everyone's* concern."

Sheriff Reed tilted his head. "You sure there's nothing you want to tell me about?"

Every muscle in my back locked up when Rachel asked, "Is there a problem?"

I turned around and sheepishly grinned at Rachel while I struggled to find the best excuse. But before I could say anything, Sheriff Reed got to his feet.

"No problem," he said. "We were just leaving."

Rachel huffed as she glared at me, then crowded into my personal space as Sheriff Reed and Dr. Shelton's departing footsteps faded away. "You've run off your first customers," she said. "I thought you said you'd waitressed before."

"I have, it's just-"

"I don't care about your excuses," she said as the frustration deepened on her face. "And I don't think Jenny will either."

"No," I said, chasing after Rachel as she headed back inside. "You can't tell her. She'll fire me."

Rachel spun around, her ponytail whipping out so far that I had to lean back to dodge it. "I know."

"What are you both doing in here? Who's manning the deck?" Jenny said, suddenly standing next to us.

"Our little Townie here just ran off three customers," Rachel said, ignoring Jenny's questions.

"You did what?" Jenny asked.

"It's not like that," I said, turning to Rachel. "But since you're at it, why don't you tell Jenny about Bill and Rob leaving *your* section?"

"That wasn't my fault," Rachel said as her face blushed. "That was because Riley..."

"Everything that happened out there was because of Riley."

Jenny shook her head and rubbed her brow. "I don't really care whose fault it is. Right now, all I am concerned with is why my two waitresses for the deck are in here."

Rachel huffed, "But-"

"But nothing," Jenny said, cutting her sentence short. "Get out there and do your job." She caught Rachel's eye. "Both of you."

Even with the summer sun blistering the deck, working with Rachel after that left a chill in the air. I never really pictured us getting pedicures together, crying on each other's shoulders about boys or anything like that, but now, it was almost confirmed that we wouldn't even be on speaking terms anytime soon. It didn't really bother me personally. But when your have a co-worker that careens down the walkway between tables, acting as if you're not standing there balancing a tray of hot food over a table of unsuspecting customers, it makes for a very long shift.

It was almost eleven o'clock when I brought the table condiments in from the deck and slid them across the window to Mel in the kitchen.

"Well, how was your first day?" he asked, smiling big enough to expose a missing tooth on the left side of his mouth.

"Could've been better, could've been worse," I said, handing him the kitchen's portion of tips.

He put it to the side, then said, "Don't let her run you off."

"Who?" I asked, already knowing the answer was Rachel.

"Miss Priss over there," he said, nodding to the booth she sat at wrapping silverware. "It may take a while, but I'm sure she'll warm up to you."

I scrunched my nose. "I'm not gonna hold my breath."

Mel laughed. "I have a feeling you're gonna fit right in with us around here." He shot another glance at Rachel as she loudly tossed the wrapped silverware into a tub. "Well, most of us anyway."

As I drove to the yellow house, I thought back to my short conversation with Sheriff Reed. What would he have said if I told him what I saw? Would he believe me?

Something about the way he didn't stop Riley the last time he went after Bill told me that Sheriff Reed knew more about what was really going on that he let on. And for whatever reason, he was letting Riley do whatever he could to keep it all a secret.

But why? Why wouldn't they want anyone to know that there was something out there? Why wouldn't they just put an article in the paper or make some kind of announcement, warning everyone to stay out of the woods, to lock their doors, to carry protection?

I mean, didn't he, as the sheriff, have some obligation to protect these people? Or was it that his loyalty to Riley was stronger than his duty to the citizens of Lost Creek?

Warm light spilled from the front windows of the yellow house and out on the dark lawn when I parked by the curb. Inside, I could see Hazel sitting in the living room, laughing with a woman that I recognized from the party last night. She had stayed by Hazel's side, much like she was doing now.

I forced my attention away from the window and started around the house, checking for Blake in the clump of trees near the property line and finding nothing but disappointment.

Where was he?

When I reached the middle of the lawn, I glanced back at the wall of glass, hoping to catch a glimpse of Blake inside, maybe waiting for my return. But all was dark.

I jerked myself from the search as I climbed the stairs to the boathouse. *This is stupid*, I thought. I didn't even know this guy, but here I was, dejected because he wasn't home. Depressed because he wasn't sitting on the deck, anticipating my return.

I didn't know what was wrong with me. This kind of attraction, this kind of infatuation, was not my norm. I mean, I wasn't one of those girls that parked in a guy's driveway until he got home. I wasn't one of those girls that called a guy every five minutes to see where he was. With every other boyfriend, I was my own person with my own life.

Plunging the key into lock, I stopped. Did I just refer to him as my boyfriend?

I shook my head, glad Blake wasn't there, since I was unsure of what I would do next. Probably propose to him or something equally humiliating.

"This is just ridiculous," I said, stepping inside.

As the door closed behind me, all the obsession with Blake crashed when pink Legos from the dreamcatcher cluttered the floor. I blinked at the orange ribbon curled beneath the beige sofa on the far side of the room, the Hello Kitty head below the large window, Dad's old tie under the bed, and the wreath broken in half with little green fibers littering the floor next to the kitchen table.

As I picked up the pieces, noting that the silver cross and plastic dragonfly were still missing, a sudden pressure built in the air. Someone had been in here and done this. That part I knew for certain. But what I didn't know was if they were still here.

I swallowed down the fear when I spotted the bathroom door cracked open about an inch. Had I left it like that? Had they done it? Where they hiding in there?

Creeping forward, I grabbed the glass bowl from the coffee table, slowly pouring the small sticks of driftwood to the floor, adding them to the mess before I raised the bowl above my head. My heart hammered so hard against my chest that if they didn't hear my footsteps, they could definitely hear the pounding as I centered myself with the paneled door.

Two quick breaths to build my nerve, then I kicked it in.

I rushed in as the door banged against the back wall then swung into my back, startling me when I stared at the closed shower curtain. A flash of a million scary movies ran through my head. There could anyone - or anything - behind there.

Another deep breath and I tightened my grip on the bowl in one hand then grabbed the shower curtain with the other. I screamed as I yanked it open, hoping to startle the intruder enough that I could react before them, then stopped when the shower was empty.

I collapsed on the side of the tub, putting the bowl by my feet then dropping my head to my hands as all the adrenaline shook through me. What was going on? Why would someone break in here? I didn't have anything to steal.

But then I turned my head and spotted my camera on the corner of my bed, the back open, the film gone.

Dazed, I drew closer, thinking that maybe when I reached it, I would see something different. I didn't.

I skimmed the bed for the missing film, but found nothing, and dropped the camera back to the mattress.

Who would do this? Who would break in to steal film? All it had on it was a few pictures of the old movie house.

Then my heart thumped against my ribs when I remembered taking a picture of the monster in the woods. Somehow someone had found out about it. And as I stood in the middle of all the muddled mess, I had a feeling that that someone was Riley Shelton.

But how? Had he seen me? Figured it out from my eavesdropping on Bill? From my conversation with Sheriff Reed?

Right now, none of that mattered. All I cared about was that now everyone was going to see Riley Shelton for what he really was.

I banged on the back door of the yellow house, rattling it in its frame. Mark answered with the same bewildered look he wore the day I arrived.

"Are you okay?" he asked as I spilled into the kitchen.

"Riley was in the boathouse," I said between shallow breaths.

"What? Did you see him?"

"No, but I know it was him."

"Riley Shelton?" Mark added with an air of disbelief.

"Yes, Riley Shelton. Tall, dark hair, miscreant."

"Are you sure?"

"What's going on?" Hazel called from the other room.

Mark announced, "Scarlett thinks someone broke into the boathouse."

"Not someone. Riley," I whispered to Mark, hoping he would yell that part too. He didn't.

"What?" another voice squawked before a collage of footsteps headed toward the kitchen. The woman I'd seen through the front window followed Hazel through the doorway. "There was a break-in in *this* neighborhood?"

Mark caught Hazel's eye. "She thinks it was Riley."

Both Hazel and her friend turned and looked at me like I had suddenly started speaking French.

"No," Hazel said, shaking her head. "His dad's my doctor."

"And besides," the woman added, "he couldn't have done that."

"And why not?" I exploded. "Because his dad's a doctor? Because he knows the sheriff? That doesn't mean anything."

"No," the woman huffed. "Because he just wouldn't do something like that. I mean, why would he?"

"Because he knew I had...something," I stuttered, realizing for the first time how ridiculous my accusations were going to sound.

"What was it?" Hazel asked.

In that moment, I wanted to say the missing item was something of much more importance, like Riley had run off with the Hope Diamond or something. But instead, all I could say was, "A roll of film."

"Like from your camera?" Hazel asked, her brow stitching together with doubt.

"Yes," I said, trying to make it sound more paramount than before.

The woman scoffed. "You seriously think Riley Shelton broke into the boathouse to steal some film?" She looked at Hazel like this was some kind of joke.

"I'm serious," I said. "It was him."

"And what was on this film?" the woman asked, failing to hide her amusement.

I put my hands up. "It doesn't matter what was on the film. The point is, it's gone and Riley took it."

Mark grabbed a flashlight from beneath the kitchen sink. "I'll go check it out. Kiki, Scarlett, stay here with Hazel."

"You can't just go out there by yourself," Hazel said, grabbing Mark's arm as he reached for the door. "What if there really is someone out there?"

Finally, someone who halfway believed me.

"I'll be fine," Mark said and kissed Hazel on the forehead. "If you see anything, just lock the door and call the sheriff."

A lot of good that'll do, I thought to myself. He would probably just tell me again that this was not my concern.

After Mark stepped out, the three of us huddled by the door, watching the beam from the flashlight bounce as he made his way toward the boathouse.

"Now what happened?" Hazel asked as her face crinkled with worry.

"Riley broke into the boathouse while I was gone."

"Why do you think that?" Kiki asked with an arched brow.

I turned to her. "Who *are* you?"

"I'm Kiki Beauchamp," she said like I should have already known who she was. "Hazel's dearest friend."

"Whatever," I said, turning back to the window.

"So are you going to answer me or just let me draw my own conclusion on what really happened?"

I huffed. "From your condescending tone, I get that you've already done that."

"It's just because I *know* the Shelton family."

"Just because you *know* a family, doesn't mean you know what they're capable of. Believe me," I said, doing everything I could not to look at Hazel, "you'd be surprised."

"Just start from the beginning," Hazel said, waving Kiki to the table. "What happened?"

"I came back from work and the place was ransacked," I said flatly.

"So you didn't see Riley?" Kiki added from the table.

When I clenched my teeth, Hazel shot Kiki a warning and she backed down. "Had you locked the door when you left for work?" Hazel asked me.

"Yes."

"Are you sure?"

I huffed. "I can remember if I locked the door or not, Hazel."

"She's just trying to be helpful," Kiki interjected.

I crossed my arms and glared at Kiki. "I know exactly what she's trying to do," I said.

Kiki didn't back down. "I don't think you do."

"Stop acting like you know me," I said.

"Then quit acting like you know her," Kiki countered.

"What's that supposed to mean?"

"Mark's coming back," Hazel said and halted the bickering. She stepped away from the door, holding one hand on her belly and the other on her back. "Well?"

"There wasn't anyone in there," Mark said.

I sighed. "I already told you that."

"Look," Mark said, "if your film is really missing, maybe you just put it in a different place."

"*If* my film is missing?"

"He didn't mean it like that, Scarlett," Hazel said in a consoling tone.

Kiki got to her feet and scoffed, "Yes, he did."

"What's wrong with you?" I snapped.

Hazel put her hand on Kiki's arm. "That's enough."

"No," Kiki said, her face twisting in anger, "she just shows up and turns your life upside-down, and *I'm* the one with the problem?"

I turned to Hazel. "Is that what you told her? That I turned your life upside down?"

Hazel's eyes darted from mine to Kiki's. That's not what I meant."

"Just like Mark didn't mean that I'd imagined my film was stolen?"

"Scarlett..."

"Look," I said, throwing my hands into the air, "I get it. This whole town refuses to see what Riley really is. And believe me, he knows it. He gets to just walk around, doing whatever it is he wants to do and *nobody* is going to say a word about it."

"That's not true," Hazel offered.

"You know what?" I said, rubbing my pounding temples. "In a few months, I'll be gone, so I don't know why I'm even bothering. All of you can live your lives as if nothing is going on, and then I'll leave this little dot on the map and you'll never have to see me again or hear my crazy stories."

Hazel shook her head. "Quit being so dramatic."

"Oh, yeah," I said with a laugh. "That's right. I'm just being hysterical. Blowing everything way out of proportion."

"Yes, you are," Kiki said.

"Shut up," I yelled. "This has nothing to do with you."

"When you hurt my friend, then I'm involved. Got it?"

"I'm the one that hurt her? Are you serious?"

They all three stared at me like I had a third eye, and as the silence built in the room, I had a feeling there was way more I was not understanding. But the parts I did understand - Mark accusing me of lying, Kiki despising me, and Hazel regretting her decision to let me stay here - was enough to push me out the door.

Chapter Seven

*I*t was very long shift at The Spot. Three days had passed since the break-in. I knew no one believed me that Riley Shelton had anything to do with it, that he had something to do with everything wrong in this town, but that didn't matter. I knew. Even Sheriff Reed shot me odd glances from a corner booth, making me feel that maybe Kiki had told him about my accusations. Again, it didn't matter. I would find a way to prove Riley's guilt.

But the disbelief and the stares didn't bother me as much as the thought of going back to the yellow house when my shift was over. Since that night, Mark and Hazel had kept to the house and their lights coming on at different intervals was the only proof I had that they were home. Yet even that was better than not knowing at all, like I had with Blake.

The house next door was just dark. Lifeless. Like he had packed up at some point that first night and just left. But even with the emptiness, I couldn't shake that tethered sensation, that connection telling me that he was still near.

With a sigh, I tossed my apron beneath the counter, waved to Mel, and headed out.

Jenny caught me just before I reached the door. "Got any big plans tonight?"

"Just a hot date with a load of laundry," I said, digging the keys from my pocket.

"Well, I'm having a little get-together at my house, if you'd like to come."

I shrugged, knowing I wouldn't know anyone there. "That's okay. But thanks."

"C'mon," Jenny said with a grin. "It's not gonna kill you to have a little fun, is it?"

The more I thought about the rest of my night, the more I could see that Jenny was right. It wasn't going to hurt. All I was giving up was a night full of unanswerable questions running through my head about the connection between Riley, the sheriff, Bill, and the thing in the woods. I could stand a night away from all that.

"All right," I said. "I'm in."

I followed Jenny's yellow Beetle down one road and then another before finally pulling onto a narrow lane a few miles out of town. Here the houses had about two acres between them, leaving large sections of darkness before the next friendly lights appeared. We pulled into a driveway, and if there hadn't been a light above the front door, I wouldn't have even known a house was nestled back there. My first thought was to turn around and go back to the yellow house. At least there, it was bright and open, not shadowy and secluded like this place. But as I rolled down my window to tell Jenny I had changed my mind, a gray Accord and a white pickup pulled in behind me, blocking me in.

"Hey, Jen!" a girl with straight black hair called out as she climbed from her car and popped her trunk.

Jenny waved back as she stood near the front of my car, waiting expectantly until I killed the engine. I followed her up the walk, all the while wiping my sweaty hands on the front of my jeans, trying to convince myself that we were *not* in the woods. We were in a neighborhood. We were safe.

"C'mon in," Jenny said, opening her front door as more cars pulled into the drive.

Inside, her house smelled lived-in, like a mixture of cooking oil and soap. On the walls were pictures of Jenny and her parents from when she was younger. The portraits steadily progressed from her as a baby through what looked like just a few years back, then stopped.

I stood in the living room, taking in the light and the walls, trying to dissolve the cloak of unease I was suddenly wearing. "Are those your parents?" I asked as Jenny disappeared down a hallway.

"Yeah," she called out.

"Are they out of town or something?" I asked, seeing no signs of them other than on the wall.

The girl from the driveway pushed through the open door, smiling at me as the box in her arms clinked with each step. I gave a quick grin, then moved out of the way when a crowd of others flooded in, moving routinely through the house, cutting off to small groups by the brick fireplace and the kitchen table.

Jenny appeared again at the end of the hall, but now in shorts and a tank top. I looked down at my own bright yellow top and hated that I was literally neon in a room full of strangers.

"My parents aren't out of town," Jenny said flatly. "They died last year."

An awkward tightness wrapped around my chest. "Oh, I'm so sorry," I stuttered.

"It's okay," she said, moving past me to the kitchen. "Hey, everyone," Jenny said, raising her hands to gain their attention. "This is Scarlett."

As if on cue, they all turned to me and smiled, some even gave a small wave. Then Jenny spewed out a string of names I forgot a millisecond after she said them. After the announcement, Jenny reached into the box the girl with the black hair brought in and pulled out a bottle of vodka. "I need a drink."

―――

It was just after midnight and I found myself in a small group at the kitchen table, listening to Becca, a girl with curly brown hair, talk about her recent five-hour attempt at being vegan.

"I even bought this *Eat More Vegan* shirt," she said. "And I swear to you by the end of the day, it smelled like bacon. I mean, what was I supposed to do? I can't resist that kind of temptation." Becca sighed and lowered her gaze to the table. "So I had to go home and change shirts before I went out for a bacon cheeseburger."

I took a sip of water as a girl next to me nodded sympathetically. But just as Becca started in on her plans to still, at least, snack vegan, the front door opened and Riley walked in with Rachel in tow.

As she waved at the group on the couch with the same enthusiasm she did with her customers, Rachel was either oblivious to my presence at this party or was ignoring me altogether. Riley, on the other hand, didn't hide his disdain as he left Rachel with the others and marched to the table, slamming his hands down hard enough to stop Becca's explanation on how Oreos were accidentally vegan.

"You're Scarlett, right?" he snarled.

I glared back at him, knowing he already knew the answer. "What's your problem?"

"Apparently, it's you."

"Seriously?" I scoffed. "I think you have bigger problems than me."

"That may be true, but right now, you're the only problem I see here."

I got to my feet. "I was invited, thank you very much."

"That's not what I meant. I've heard you've been going around saying things."

I leaned forward and gritted my teeth. "Nothing that's not true."

Riley saw the sudden audience. "Why don't we talk about this somewhere more private?"

"I don't think we have anything to talk about," I said, shaking my head.

But before I knew it, Riley grabbed my arm from across the table and pulled me toward the back door. "Oh, I think we do."

"Let go of me," I demanded, squirming against his grip. But it was pointless, as Riley opened the door with his free hand and pushed me outside with the other.

"Start talking," he said, blocking the only exit, other than through the woods. And there was no way I was going through there.

"Why? So you can shut me up like you did Bill?"

Riley crossed his arms and tilted his head as if he were trying to read my mind to find out exactly what I knew. "The thing is, Scarlett," Riley said slowly as he chose his words, "Bill's crazy. Everyone knows that."

"Is he, Riley?" I countered. "Something tells me that you don't think he's crazy at all."

"And why do you think that?"

"Because you're doing everything you can to keep him quiet about what's really going on in Lost Creek. You've done it with Bill and his story, and now with me and my film."

Riley's irritation relaxed as he laughed, "That's what this is all about? Some stupid film?" He pushed out a long sigh. "Okay, okay. This was just some big misunderstanding."

I blinked at him. "There's no misunderstanding," I said incredulously. "I know I'm just a Townie and all, but where I come from, breaking and entering is a crime, no matter if you're friends with the sheriff or not."

In the dim illumination coming from the porch lamp, I could see a small smirk pull at Riley's face. "Look, I don't know what you *think* you know, but-"

"I know it was you."

"Do you now?"

"Yeah," I said smugly.

"And what proof do you have? Did you see me? Did I leave my ID there? What?"

I stood there, silent.

"That's what I thought," Riley said with a simper. "You are so far from knowing what's really going on. Your film disappearing doesn't have anything to do with Bill or-" But then in the next breath, all the seriousness returned to his face. "Wait. What was on the film?"

"Like you don't know."

"I don't, Scarlett," he said so convincingly that, for a moment, I believed him.

"Yeah right," I said, fighting the urge to slap the feign look of confusion from his face. I ran my hand through my hair. "You think you're so...so..."

"So what?" Riley asked.

"So above it all," I finally choked out. "And you're not. Sooner or later, everyone's gonna know the truth."

It was just a millisecond, but I saw surprise flash across Riley's face before he composed himself again. "What have you seen?"

"Why? So you can shut me up too?" I said, shaking my head. "I don't think so."

"I'm serious, Scarlett," Riley said, stepping forward, his necklace bouncing a single time against his chest. "Tell me."

I held his gaze, wanting to see the panic in his eyes when he realized I wasn't going to play nice. "We both know what I've seen."

But the fear he held didn't seem to be for his personal safety, but for mine. "Listen to me," Riley said, gripping my arms with much more force as he had before. "You don't know what's going on."

"I may not have proof - thanks to you - but I will. And when I do-"

"Don't pursue this," Riley said, cutting me off. "You're gonna get yourself hurt."

"Is that a threat?" I challenged, trying in vain to free myself.

Riley's passion turned solemn as he leaned in, his breath on my face. "That's not a threat, Scarlett. It's a promise."

The back door burst open and Riley dropped his hold on me when he saw that Rachel stood there, eyeing us both. "What's going on out here?"

"Nothing," I said as I dug the keys from my pocket and pushed past Rachel. "I was just leaving."

"Don't go looking for trouble," Riley called out.

But as I hurried through the living room and out the front door, I had a feeling I had already found it.

Chapter Eight

Last night's conversation with Riley hadn't made me feel as great as I imagined it would have. Maybe because nothing had changed. I still had no physical proof that anything was going on and Riley was still getting away with it. But now Riley knew he was being watched and that fact gave me a small sliver of satisfaction.

I lugged my bag of laundry down the stairs, hating that it wasn't even noon and I was already sweating by the time I reached the lawn. Through the back windows of the yellow house, I could see Hazel in the kitchen with mixing bowls lining the countertops.

In the middle of the lawn, I stopped and watched her move. It was familiar and new in the same breath. She had probably done this a million times before, starting in the little house we grew up in, then here, in her new life. Her surrounding changed, but her movements, her actions were the same. I wondered if she ever thought back to those days, when I would sit on a bar stool and watch the flour puff out in a little cloud when she added it to the bowl. Did she miss those moments of eating raw cookie dough as we talked about nothing?

Probably not, I thought to myself as I lugged my bag back onto my shoulder and headed to my car.

The laundromat was empty, but the hum and heat of used machines filled the air. Near the back, I found two empty washers next to each other and loaded them up with clothes and detergent, jammed my quarters into the slots, and started the machine. I hunkered down in a hard plastic chair and grabbed an abandoned magazine that was six months old to try to kill the time.

As I neared the middle of the magazine, dryer number four buzzed and slowly came to a stop. I looked at the door of the laundromat, assuming the owner of the contents would come pushing through to finish up. But after a long minute, no one came in, so I moved my attention back to an article about how to lose ten pounds in two weeks.

Eventually, the thrum of the washers I was using died and I grabbed a nearby cart, throwing the wet clothes into it. I pushed it over to the dryers, still wondering about the whereabouts of the operator of dryer number four. I had just started my dryer when Bill Dickerson walked in and headed straight for the unclaimed dryer.

Yanking the door open, he picked up a few pieces of clothing, then sighed before slamming the door and adding more quarters to restart the machine.

"These things are a rip-off, you know?" he said to me as he watched the clothes begin to circle in the glass window. "They never dry on a single cycle. You have to pay two, sometimes three, times to get the job done right."

My heart raced as all the questions I wanted to ask

jumbled in my brain, threatening to gush out in no particular order. But I swallowed back the nervousness and smiled. "I've seen you at The Spot, haven't I?"

Bill thinned his eyes like he was trying to recall my face, then he returned the grin. "You're that new girl, aren't you?"

"Yeah," I said, stepping toward him with an outstretched hand. "I'm Scarlett."

"Bill Dickerson," he said. His hand was cool and soft as it wrapped around mine. "Nice to meet you."

"I saw you on my first day," I said, trying to sound nonchalant.

"Oh, yeah?" he said with a laugh. "Hope I didn't give you too hard of a time."

"No," I said, "I don't remember you because of that. I was working out on the deck when Riley Shelton bothered you and your friend."

Bill's friendly demeanor faded from his face. "Is this some kind of joke?" he said, his voice lower than before. "Are you making fun of me?"

"No," I said, shaking my head. "I just had some questions, that's all."

Bill looked consumed by uneasiness as he quickly glanced out the window at the front street. "I don't think this is anything you want to get mixed up with, missy."

"Look," I said, keeping my voice light and even, "all I need are a few answers."

"I'll tell you right now, I don't have any answers. Not to this."

I took another step toward him slowly and smiled.

"But you know what's going on, don't you?"

I could tell from the shift in his gaze, he knew something. But instead of telling me, Bill just shook his head and backed away. "Riley told me if I told anyone..." Bill said, letting his sentence die.

"Are you scared of Riley?" I asked. "Did he threaten to hurt you if you said anything?"

Bill continued to shake his head. "Like I said, miss, this ain't nothing you want anything to do with."

When Bill looked at the door, I had a feeling he was about to make a run for it and I would lose this opportunity to find out the truth. I took in a sharp breath and blurted, "I've seen it too."

Bill snapped back to the present, his eyes wide as he stared at me. "What'd you say?"

"I said I've seen it," I repeated. "The black mist, the yellow eyes, the claws."

Bill crowded me, fear and concern racing across his face. "I don't know how else to tell you," he whispered, "but you need to leave this alone. Things aren't what you think they are in this town."

"What do you mean? What is that thing?"

Bill backed away from me again, shaking his head. "You wouldn't believe me if I told you."

"C'mon," I said with a slight laugh to try to ease the tension. "What is it? Some kind of science experiment gone wrong or something?"

"That ain't no science experiment," Bill said with a quiver. "That thing out there is heaven and hell, biblical stuff."

"What?" I asked, certain I had missed something.

"Are you not listening to anything I'm sayin'?"

"I, I heard you," I said, stuttering. "I just don't understand what you're trying to tell me."

Bill stepped toward me, his skin ashy white. "I ain't *trying* to tell you nothing. What I'm saying is that thing's a demon."

I squinted at him in disbelief. "You can't be serious."

"I knew you wouldn't believe me," Bill said with a long-suffering sigh.

"It's not that I don't believe you," I fumbled as I lied. "It's just...I don't know...a lot to take in all at once."

"Like I said, this ain't nothing you want to get mixed up with. But you wanted answers and now you know. Now you're like me."

That comparison really didn't make me feel any better.

"Okay," I said, holding up my hands. "Let's just say it's true-"

"It *is* true."

"All right," I said slowly. "Then why hasn't anybody else seen it?"

Bill looked out the front window again and said, "Because it changes."

"Changes?" I asked. "Changes how?"

Aggravation was thick in Bill's glare. "One minute it looks like you and me, then the next minute, it looks like... well, you know what it looks like."

"How does it do that?"

"I don't know," Bill yelled. "I already told ya I don't

have answers. All I know is what I've just said."

My attention shifted to his shoulder. "Well, what about your arm? How'd that happen?"

"It probably knew I was snooping around, asking questions," Bill said, shaking his head as he gripped his arm. "Probably did this as a warning to shut me up."

I didn't know what to say.

"But if I were you, I'd just forget what ya saw," Bill said slowly as Riley's Jeep passed in front of the laundry mat.

"That's gonna be hard to do."

When the front window was clear again, Bill pushed out an agitated laugh, tore open the dryer and pulled out his still damp clothes, shoving them into a bag. "I've already said too much."

"Don't go," I said, trying to stop him. "Just tell me what Riley has to do with all this. Why he's trying to keep it all a secret?"

Bill stopped. "Riley's got his own reason for that."

"Like what?"

"I've already told ya," Bill yelled as he pulled open the door. "Things aren't what you think they are in Lost Creek."

I couldn't get Bill's words out of my head. I wanted nothing more than to believe that everyone had been right and he was crazy, but the way he spoke about whatever this thing was, was so lucid, so clear. I thought back to that first night on the road, and that day in the forest. I had known, just as I knew now, somewhere deep inside, that

that thing wasn't of this world.

Things like that don't really exist, I tried to tell myself again as I parked in front of the yellow house and unloaded my laundry.

But as I made it around to the side yard, something in the air felt different, heavier, and I slowed my gait, glancing at the small shadows behind the bushes, jerking my attention to the birds fluttering overhead.

At first, I thought I was just freaking myself out. But when Hazel's scream billowed from the yellow house, I bounded up the back steps and tore through the screen door. I spotted Hazel leaning against the counter, gripping her belly.

"What's wrong?" I said, stepping toward her, but then stopped when I caught a glimpse of something dark out of the corner of my eye.

I steadied my breath as I tried to convince myself there was nothing there, that I was still just all worked up from the conversation with Bill. But even before I turned to look, I knew, just like in the forest, I wasn't alone.

A demon was here.

Chapter Nine

I still wanted to believe that Bill was crazy. That what he said was just as insane as it sounded coming from his mouth. But now as three dark strands broke from the demon's body and drifted across the floor, one toward me and the others toward Hazel, I knew two things for certain: every word Bill said was true, and Hazel and I were going to die.

I stood there, frozen with fear, frozen with uncertainty, as the hazy tentacles wrapped around Hazel like an octopus pulling in its prey. Tears streamed from my eyes as I realized I had done this to her. I had asked too many questions and brought this thing here, looking for me.

Hazel's knees buckled as she gripped her belly with one hand and continued to clench the nearby counter with the other.

"Just leave her alone," I screamed, but my plea only seemed to excite the demon as it expanded up the wall, stretching itself taller.

With every breath, the air grew colder and a pressure built in the room. I gripped my thighs, bracing myself against the mounting weight, watching the appendage continue to reach out for me.

There was no way out of this. There was no flash of the camera to distract the demon, there was no one coming to the rescue. And as I dared another glance into its distorted face, I could see that it knew this as well.

But something Bill had uttered replayed in my head: *That thing out there is heaven and hell, biblical stuff.*

"God help me," I whispered with what I thought would be my last breath.

Then as I waited to be crushed by this spiritual monster, I felt a small seed of courage take root in the pit of my stomach. I raised my head, blinking back the terror that threatened to blind me, and stepped over the tendril of darkness toward my sister. The heaviness in the room grew thicker, making every step feel like I was walking against the entire current of the ocean.

But my focus stayed on Hazel while she fought her own battle to stay on her feet as the wisps of evil climbed her like a wicked vine on a trellis, weakening her. I gained another step, then readied for the next wave of pressure.

After what seemed like hours of battle to gain a few feet, I stretched my shaky fingertips toward Hazel's now pale skin, then used the last bit of strength I had to close the distance. As my skin touched hers, a shriek I had only heard in my nightmares exploded from the demon and pierced the smothered silence as it pulled its appendages back and shattered the crushing pressure building on the room. In the last second, I lunged forward, breaking Hazel's fall and collecting her in my arms as her eyes fluttered and closed.

I turned back to the corner and found that the demon had turned to a dark mist, but even in the shadows, its yellow eyes tapered into small slits as it stared down at me. I wrapped my arms tighter around Hazel, burying her head beneath my arms, shielding her from whatever wrath this thing was about to unleash. But as I braced myself, closing my eyes and holding my breath, nothing happened.

I don't know how long I stayed there - a minute, an hour, a day - afraid to look up, afraid to breathe, afraid to move. But when something gripped my shoulder, I jerked back my elbow and knocked it away.

Metal bowls clanged against the tile as I turned to see Blake pulling himself from the floor, holding his hand to his busted jaw. "What was that for?" he said, his voice thick with friction.

"I...I..." I said, stuttering with confusion.

He pushed past me to Hazel's side. "What happened here?" When I didn't answer, he looked at me from over his shoulder. "Talk to me," he said. "What happened?"

"There was something..." I looked back at the empty corner, then at Hazel still sprawled across the floor while tears blurred my vision.

Slowly, Hazel stirred and she glanced at Blake, then at me in between heavy blinks. She moved to sit up, but Blake put his hand on her shoulder and kept her where she was.

"What happened?" she asked with a voice that sounded too small for her body.

"We were hoping you could tell us," Blake said.

Hazel paused for a long moment, like she was trying to recall a distant dream, then shook her head. "I don't know."

But Blake wasn't dissuaded and moved his body to shield his next question from reaching Hazel. "What do you know about this?" he whispered.

The way he looked at me told me that he already knew the gist of what had transpired here. But as I teetered between what I should say, Mark arrived home and spotted us all on the floor in the kitchen.

"What's going on?" he said with his keys still in his hand.

"I think I fainted," Hazel said, trying to sit up again. This time Blake didn't try to stop her. Instead, he got to his feet and stepped back, letting Mark take control.

"Just stay there, sweetheart," Mark said to Hazel, pulling a phone from his pocket with one hand while smoothing back her dark hair with the other.

"Let's give them room," Blake said, helping me to my feet before holding open the back door.

Outside the air was thick and hard to breathe as I leaned against the house next to the screen door. Blake rested against the porch railing across the way, eyeing me as I pretended to listen in on Mark as he called the doctor.

"Now do you want to tell me what's going on?" Blake said, breaking the silence.

Slowly, I shifted my eyes to him. "What am I supposed to say?"

He pushed from the railing and stepped toward me, making my heart race. "How about the truth?"

"It's not that simple," I said while my head whirled with doubt.

"Sure it is," Blake said as he looked through the screen door toward Hazel in the kitchen and then back at me. "You just open your mouth and say it."

I was jolted when Mark pushed open the door and was suddenly beside me. "Dr. Shelton wants me to take Hazel to the hospital. Are you coming?"

Before I could say anything, Blake answered, "We'll be right behind you."

In a few seconds, the house fell quiet and Blake started with the questioning again. "Just tell me what happened. What did you see?"

I shook my head. "I don't know."

"You don't know or you don't want to tell me?"

"What difference does it make? It still happened," I said. "Hazel's still going to the hospital."

"Just take it easy," Blake said, showing his palms. "I'm just trying to figure out if you're okay or not."

"How am I supposed to answer that?" I said with a shaky laugh. "I don't know what's going on. I don't understand-"

"What you're seeing?" Blake said flatly, finishing my sentence.

All I had was silence.

A pang of struggle engulfed Blake's expression as he cocked his head, observing me. "If it makes you feel any better, you're handling it better than most," he said carefully.

"Handling what?" I said.

"Your glimpse."

I pushed out a slow breath, fighting a wave of nausea. "Into what?"

"The unseen realm," Blake said as he furrowed his brow. "Some people can't even utter a word until months later. But you, you're strong."

"I don't know about that," I said, shaking my head as I paced the length of the porch. "I don't really believe any of this. I mean, this stuff doesn't happen. Not in real life."

"Can you honestly say that now?"

An answer was pointless.

"What are you?" I quipped. "Some kind of spiritual counselor or something? Here to help me cope?"

A hint of amusement pulled at Blake's lips. "No."

I suddenly felt on edge. "You aren't with that team in there, are you?" I asked, nodding to the kitchen, trying to hide that fact that I was terrified.

Another slight grin that, in normal circumstances would have made me blush, but now it just kind of irritated me. This wasn't a laughing matter. This was life-altering, whether I was handling it satisfactorily in Blake's eyes or not.

"Look, I don't have time for this," I said, pushing past Blake and down the stairs. "My sister's on the way to the hospital and I need to check on her."

Rage and doubt swirled inside me, fueling every footstep that put distance between me and Blake. Yet when I reached the side yard, certain I could find a reasonable explanation to all of this once I had time to think, the scope of my world narrowed to Blake standing on the cobblestone path.

"How?" I fumbled, turning back to the elevated porch, finding it empty. "You were just there, and now..."

But Blake remained still and silent as if letting my mind meld with this new reality while my old one fell away.

"What are you?" I whispered so softly that I barely heard my own voice.

I don't know what I expected Blake to say, what I expected him to do. But when I blinked and he was suddenly in front of me with just a sliver of space between us, my breath caught in my chest. His hand slipped perfectly into mine and the veil of shelter he had provided that day I'd first met him washed over me, deflecting every thought of worry, every pang of uncertainty I felt.

I sank deeper, letting myself fall, letting myself believe, as I gazed up into Blake's beautiful eyes, taking in each golden fleck that shimmered from an unknown light.

Blake leaned in, his voice as soft and warm as his flesh against mine, and whispered, "Scarlett, I'm your only hope."

***

Blake had seemed so normal - so human - that if I hadn't witnessed his blinding speed, hadn't felt his calming touch, hadn't cradled this supernatural connection toward him, I wouldn't believe he was anything other than that. But now, there were so many questions, and as I tried to sort them all out in my head, they just shifted back into a tangled mess leaving me staring at Blake as he drove us to the hospital.

"There are rules," Blake warned suddenly. "First, no one can know what you've seen. It puts people in unnecessary danger."

Great, I thought to myself, cringing on the inside. So much for that one.

"Second, you can't tell others about me," Blake said, cutting his eyes to me for a moment, before pulling into the hospital parking lot. "It puts *me* in danger."

I nodded.

"And third," Blake said as he put the car in park, "you can't go looking for this thing. That puts *you* in danger." He unexpectedly took my chin in his hand to gain my full attention. "That's the most important one, Scarlett. Do you understand?"

"I got it," I said, squeaking on the last word.

Hazel and Mark were already in an examination room waiting to see Dr. Shelton, leaving Blake and I exiled to a small waiting area with stiff chairs and old magazines. I sat by a long window and looked out at the parking lot, wondering what happened to the world I used to know; a world where people were just people. But now it seemed as if even the trees and sky were different.

Two hours passed without a word between Blake and me, but it wasn't an awkward silence. It was more of a necessary one, since words seemed so inadequate in light of everything else. Even the mental checklist I crossed off every day, preparing for college in the fall, seemed trivial now, like worrying about what shampoo you're going to use the night before your first skydive.

But even with the reassurance I felt with Blake, I still wished I had a way to change the channel in my brain as it looped back to the kitchen, back to the demon, forcing me to relive the horrendous event. I closed my eyes and slouched in my chair, trying to relax the tightening in my chest and calm the beating of my heart that pounded so loudly it drowned out the quiet pages from the overhead intercom. Yet as I stayed there, trying in vain to think of anything other than this afternoon, something familiar in the mass tugged at my subconscious, some detail I was trying to pinpoint, but missed.

"Here you go," Blake said, jerking me from my thoughts, as he stood in front of me with a cup of coffee. "I thought you could use a cup."

"Thanks."

Blake took the seat next to me, his warm skin brushing against my arm. I put the coffee on the table next to me as my eyelids grew heavy and I sank beneath that invisible veil of sanctuary Blake lavished on me. I had just felt myself plummet into slumber when Mark's voice broke through.

"She's doing better," Mark said, jolting me awake. But as I got to my feet and my eyes cleared away the curtain of sleep, Mark's forehead was still crinkled with worry. "Dr. Shelton wants to keep her for observation, so..."

"So you're staying here tonight?" I said, finishing his sentence.

Mark nervously rubbed the back of his neck. "Yeah."

The fact that Hazel would be away from the house and under constant supervision of the hospital staff came as a huge relief. Although I wasn't sure what they could do if that thing decided to show up here.

I pushed the thought away and asked, "Can I see Hazel before I go?"

"Yeah," Mark said, "of course."

The evening news played softly on the TV in Hazel's room. As I got a better look at her, the light blue blanket draped across her belly made it look like it'd grown ten pounds since this afternoon. She lazily clicked off the TV and turned to us with a sleepy smile.

"Hey," she said, dragging out the word to three syllables. "There you are."

I wasn't sure who she was talking to, but figured it wasn't me since she smiled at Mark and rubbed her belly. A silenced engulfed the room and Mark looked at me expectantly like I was supposed to say something to fill the void.

"How're you feeling?" I asked, surprised by how loud my voice sounded.

"Good," she said as she closed her heavy eyes.

Mark leaned into my ear. "They've got her on some medication."

I stepped closer to her bed and glanced at the monitors beeping next to her. A small part of me still battled to cling to the bitterness of everything wrong between us. But seeing her like this, knowing why she was here and how close I had come to losing her forever, I found myself not wanting to breathe, not wanting to blink, not wanting to do anything that moved time forward.

"You scared me," I whispered to her, moving a strand

of dark hair from her forehead.

"Don't be scared, Scarlett," she whispered back and grabbed my hand.

In a breath, I was small again, looking to my big sister, waiting her to tell me everything was going to be okay. But instead, she closed her eyes and drifted to sleep. I gripped Hazel's hand tighter, realizing I didn't care if she comforted me or not. All I wanted now was to capture this moment and tuck in my pocket to remind myself years later, that for one fleeting moment, things were okay between Hazel and me. That somehow in the midst of everything wrong, we found a way back to each other, if only for a short time.

"Visiting hours are almost over," a nurse called from the doorway a little while later.

Blake lingered by the door until I passed, then followed me out. "She's gonna be okay," he said.

I smiled politely, hoping he was right.

We had almost reached the end of the hallway when I heard Mark running to catch up with us. "What's wrong?" I asked, looking past him toward Hazel's room to see if doctors were rushing in.

"Nothing," he said in between breaths. "I just thought that maybe you should call and tell your mom that Hazel's in the hospital."

My throat closed up as I blinked at him, trying to find the words to tell him no and that I was pretty sure that was a job designated for the spouse. But then Mark patted my shoulder in an appreciative matter, taking my silence as acceptance to his request.

With everything that had happened, I found that as Blake drove me back to the yellow house, I had not yet reached my threshold of anxiety. A thousand scenarios played in my head at the thought of calling Mom. Maybe she would be very blasé about the entire thing, like I was just telling her about an article I read in the newspaper. Or maybe she would just ask me to keep her updated on what was happening. But even as I tried to convince myself that these were valid possibilities, I knew what was really going to happen: she was going to freak out and find a way to blame it all on me. Sighing, I decided I would just call her later.

The neighborhood was quiet as I climbed from the car. Blake met up with me at the cobblestone path and gripped my hand as a cool breeze swept across the lawn, carrying away my troubles. I didn't care about what Mom was going to say when I eventually called her. I didn't worry about Hazel in the hospital. I wasn't even concerned that I had seen a demon. All I thought about was the way Blake's hand encompassed mine, holding it, protecting it, shielding it.

"How long are you planning to stay in Lost Creek?" Blake asked softly as we walked across the back lawn.

"Until the fall," I said, feeling the muscles in my neck relax.

"And then what?"

I shrugged. "Then, hopefully, off to college."

"What's the *hopefully* part? Are you still waiting on something?"

"I've been accepted," I said. "Just a little short on

funds."

"Ah," he said, nodding. "Is that why you're working at The Spot?"

I glanced at him, wondering how he knew that, since I was certain I hadn't mentioned it. But when he returned the look, I had a feeling he knew more about me than just where I worked.

"How did you know to find us in the kitchen?" I asked.

Blake paused as he considered his response. "Let's just say I've had an eye on you for a while."

"But why me?"

Blake just held his secret behind a charming smile as we reached the base of the stairs. "Let's get you inside," he said gently, starting me on the ascent.

Grains of sand scratched the boards beneath my feet as the wood whined, and when I reached the third step, Blake slipped his hand from mine, bringing me back to the world of the living, back to the world of gloom and misery. But I kept my focus on the door at the top of the stairs, fighting the urge to find his hand again and fall back beneath the veil he graciously provided.

At the landing, I turned, expecting to see Blake climbing the stairs behind me, but instead, he stood anchored in the grass. "What are you doing?" I asked.

He pushed his hands deep into his pockets and then turned toward his house. "Have a good night, Scarlett," he called out over his shoulder.

"Wait. Where are you going? What happened to all that stuff about you being my only hope?" I said, scurrying halfway down the stairs. "Aren't you going to, at least, check inside?"

Blake paused, his back to me, but even in the dim light emitted from the boathouse, I could see the small muscles in his neck tense. He turned just enough that his eyes caught mine. "You'll be okay tonight," he said, then started on his departure again.

"How do you know that?" I said as he slipped deeper into the darkness.

But just as before, Blake held onto his secrets and kept walking. A part of me wanted to run after him and demand he stand guard, demand he stay with me in case that thing showed up again. Yet as I watched him abandon the comforts of his house and start down the shoreline, something told me he was doing what he could to keep me safe. Even if it meant going after the demon alone.

Chapter Ten

Rule number three, I kept reminding myself, listening to my inner voice argue that I wouldn't technically be going out in search of the demon, but for Blake.

It's the same thing.
No, it's not.
Yes, it is.

I wanted to scream.

Slowly, the tips of the trees and the sky broke apart in a blaze of glory as a new day dawned. But there was still no sign of Blake. No evidence that he was okay.

What was I supposed to do now? There was no discussion about this in Blake's list of rules. There was no timeframe on when he was supposed to be back or when I should start to worry – even though I started that the moment he disappeared around the bend. But I didn't even know that was something I needed to ask since I didn't know he was going until I saw him walking away.

And by then, it was too late.

Exhausted from the constant vigil, I moved the couch across the floor to the window, the commotion sounding explosive in the silence. I grabbed the blanket from the bed and curled up on the end of the couch, propping my head on the arm, staring out into the waking world, waiting to see Blake again.

✼

My eyes shot open when a strange swooshing sound came from the other side of the door. In a panic, I kicked off the blanket and rushed outside, squinting against the sudden brightness. I blinked as I tried to see any signs of Blake through the windows next door.

"About time you got up," a woman said behind me, knocking me from my search, as the swooshing began again.

"What are you doing?" I snarled at Kiki sweeping the deck, her hair coiffed like she was going to an opera.

With a huff, she stopped and wiped her brow with the back of her hand. "What you should be doing," she said, shoving the broom toward me. "This place looks horrible."

I left the broom hanging between us. "This isn't my mess. I didn't do this."

She snorted. "Yeah, right."

"I didn't," I said, bending down to look at the grainy substance more closely. "What is this stuff?"

"It's salt," Kiki said curtly.

It was everywhere, dusting the railing, coating the floorboards, there was even salt piled in a thick layer above the door and windows.

"How'd it get here?"

Kiki propped the broom against the wall and dusted off her hands. "How am I supposed to know? You're the one that lives here, remember?"

"I know, but-"

"Just get it cleaned up before it ruins the deck," Kiki said. "Salt's very destructive."

Baffled by the entire situation, I didn't even argue with her and grabbed the broom. I pushed the salt through the small cracks between the boards, watching it sprinkle down into the dark waters of the lake. But I stopped when Kiki was halfway down the staircase. "Wait. What are you doing here anyway? Other than being my sister's housekeeping inspector."

"Oh, they're keeping Hazel for another couple of days," Kiki said as if suddenly remembering. "Mark couldn't get a hold of you and wanted me to come by and see if you'd called your mother yet." After a moment of silence, she added, "Have you?"

"Not yet."

Kiki had her hand on her hip and a smirk on her face as she marched back up the stairs. "You know Mark and Hazel have enough to worry about. The least you could do is call your mother like he asked."

"I don't get service out here, so..."

Sighing, Kiki fumbled with her key ring, then slapped a key on the railing. "You can use their phone," she snapped. "I'm sure they wouldn't mind."

Great.

"I'll call her after I finish cleaning up this mess," I said. "Is there anything else?"

"Oh," Kiki said, handing me an envelope she pulled from her back pocket.

"What is it?" I said, cautiously taking it, wondering if maybe it was a formal eviction notice and Kiki was just there to revel in the moment.

"Just open it."

I thought about just throwing the unopened envelope on the ground and storming inside, but instead I let out a pained breath and slid my finger beneath the pink embossed sticker. I couldn't help but glance at Kiki before I opened it. There was a sudden excitement in Kiki as she pushed a fallen strand of her golden hair behind her pearl studded ear.

"It's a baby shower," Kiki squealed before I had time to read it, then gave three small claps before grasping her hands together and bringing them to her chest as if her life's work was finally complete. "It's still a week away, but..."

"I have to work," I said, deflating her excitement with four little words.

"At that little grease-trap The Spot?" Kiki snarled.

"At least it's a job," I countered.

Kiki rolled her eyes. "For now."

"What's that supposed to mean?"

"Let's just say its future is looking a bit dim."

"Whatever," I said. "You don't know anything."

Kiki snipped. "Well, I know that when I was standing in line at the bank, Francis Silverstein told me it's a prime piece of real estate and the place is such a dump, it'd almost be better for The Spot to just cut their losses and sell it already."

"There's nothing wrong with that place. It quirky, yeah, but it's not a dump."

"No offense, Scarlett, but you're new to town and you just don't see it," Kiki said as she twisted her face in disagreement. "I think that girl Jenny just needs to face the facts."

"I might be new in town, but I have eyes. I've worked in some horrible places before-"

"I bet you have," Kiki laughed.

I glared at her and Kiki masked her amusement. "It's Jenny's livelihood."

"Look," Kiki said with an annoyed tone. "I didn't come here to talk to you about The Spot. I came here to tell you about Hazel and invite you to her baby shower."

"And I already told you, I have to work."

Kiki glared. "It's in a week, Scarlett," she said, eyeing me over. "And if your mom can manage to change a few things around to make it out here, I'm sure you can do the same thing."

"You invited my mother?" I seethed.

"Of course, I did. This is her first grandchild," Kiki said. "I'm sure she'd want to be here."

Kiki had a point. But what she didn't understand, just like Mark hadn't, was that our family was not the warm, fuzzy, come-and-visit-when-you-can kind. It was the I'll-move-and-try-to-never-see-you-again kind. And in that rare instance when we found each other again and were gathered under the same roof, it was practically guaranteed to be a disaster. Sure, Mom would come, but not without outbursts and upsets. She would fling our dirty secrets upon unsuspecting guests, cause a scene about not being invited to the wedding. Then before the day was over, there would be some sort of episode with tears, indiscernible rants, stumbling, and something - usually valuable or sentimental - broken.

That was something I wanted nothing to do with.

"And like I already told you," I said, letting the envelope fall to the ground and into the salt, "I have to work."

Kiki picked it up and dusted it off. "What is wrong with you?" Kiki asked, perching her manicured hands on her hips again.

"There's nothing wrong with me," I said. "I'm just not going."

"Because of your mom."

"Yes, because of my mom. And what difference does it make if I'm there or not?"

"She's your sister, Scarlett," Kiki clipped.

"And?"

"And you should *want* to be there."

I let out a disbelieving laugh. "*She* doesn't want me there. Believe me."

"Why would you say that?" Kiki asked, raising her hands and motioning to the boathouse. "I think it's pretty clear that she wants you around."

"Whatever," I spat. "You don't know anything about Hazel and me. If you did, you'd take that invitation back and throw it away yourself."

"Well, I know your sister and I know how hurt she was when you didn't come to her wedding. And I know how hurt she'll be if you don't come to the shower. Especially when the only excuse you have is that you have to work. Come on, you could at least try to think of something more original," Kiki scoffed. "Why not just tell her you having a root canal that day?"

"Wait? What are you talking about?" I asked, shaking my head. "She didn't invite me to her wedding."

Kiki's face grew hard with skepticism. "Yes, she did. I mailed the invitations myself," she said. "So if you didn't get it, it wasn't because of Hazel."

As her words seeped into my brain, the fight within me fizzled out, leaving me standing there with nothing to say.

"You mean a lot to her," Kiki said after an awkward silence filled the air between us. "And for whatever reason, God's brought you two back together. In my experience, you only get so many chances to make things right. So don't waste this opportunity to fix things with her."

She placed the envelope on the railing, then moved the key on top of it to keep it pinned down before turning to leave. As I watched her walk away, I realized that Bill had been right about this town being full of things that weren't what they seemed.

Sweat dripped down my back as I worked at getting every last grain of salt from the deck, all the while, my brain jumped from wondering where Blake was to scrolling through the list of excuses on why I couldn't or shouldn't call Mom. I mean, what was the point? Hazel would be out in a few days, and even if Mom wanted to come and see her while she was in the hospital - which I knew she wouldn't - by the time she got here, it'd be too late. Plus, I could just wait to tell her at the baby shower and watch her face as she found out *I* withheld news about Hazel from her.

But still, I knew, even with all my excuses, all my plans at getting even, I still had to do it. I still had to call Mom. I marched across the lawn, checking Blake's house once more and finding it still empty before I climbed the back steps to the yellow house. As I plunged the key into the lock on the back door, I hoped, for an instant, that Kiki had pulled the wrong one from her key ring. No such luck.

I moved quickly through the kitchen, keeping my eyes from the corner that had held the demon the day before, then found Hazel's cell phone on the coffee table in the living room. I perched myself on the edge of the couch, rubbing my sweaty hands on the top of my legs, telling myself that it was stupid to be so nervous.

It's just Mom, I thought. *I've talked to her for eighteen years.*

But as I stared at the phone, still resting on the coffee table in front of me, I knew I had never spoken to her after leaving in such a horrible way. I wondered if she would try to explain her side of the situation and tell me why she wasn't able to stand up against Frank when he'd done what he'd done. I wondered if she would tell me she kicked him out because of it. I wondered if she would confess about not telling me about Hazel getting married and now the baby, or if she would wait until I brought it up. But more than anything, I wondered if she'd ask me to come back.

It was that thought that kept me from picking up the phone. Because no matter how much I hated what had happened, no matter how much I tried to tell myself that I was never going to set foot in that house again, a part of me missed it. Its scent, its familiarities. The feeling of home.

I had dialed nine of the ten numbers four different times and then hung up, before I finally pushed the fear into my belly and pressed the last digit. The anticipation of hearing her voice, raspy and tired, grew with every ring. Maybe she wouldn't even pick up. Maybe it would go to her voicemail and I could just leave the information and not have to speak to her. But then my breath caught in my chest when the ringing stopped and a man answered.

"Who is this?" I asked.

"You're the one who called," he said, the last word gravelly and harsh.

"Is this Frank?"

"Who's this?"

Bile rose in my throat, but I choked it back. "This is Scarlett."

"Scarlett," he said with a smirk in his voice. "Have you called to apologize?"

"What? No," I said. "I didn't do anything wrong."

"Are you sure about that?" he added.

"Yes, I'm sure."

He pushed out an exasperated sigh, then said, "You would think that, wouldn't you?"

"What's that supposed to mean?"

"Let's just say I'm not the one making *my* mother cry

herself to sleep every night."

I doubted he even had a mother, and if he did, I was almost certain they were not on speaking terms, making his evaluation of my relationship with Mom laughable. But still his words were just as relentless as when he knocked me into the bookshelf that night I left, although this time, the damage was much more destructive, much more permanent.

"Is she there?" I said, fighting to keep my voice flat and even.

There was a silence on the other end, then a shuffle, before finally Mom got on the phone. "Scarlett?"

In that moment, all the emotions I thought I had left behind lodged themselves in my throat, suffocating me.

"Hello?" she said and I could almost see the way her forehead crinkled.

"I'm here," I said, my voice sounding too small to have come from my lips. Then I just sat there, waiting. For what, I wasn't certain. But I wanted something more than the quiet that filled the line. More than the emptiness that now consumed me. More than Mom waiting for me to reach out to her.

After a few moments, I knew that whatever it was I was looking for was not going to be found today. Not with Mom. Not with this absent conversation.

"Hazel's in the hospital," I said and finally heard a reaction from Mom's end of the line.

It was odd, listening to her cry. I tried to imagine that was what she sounded like when, according to the exaggerations of Frank, she cried herself to sleep over me. But

I knew none of that was true. She didn't miss me. If she did, she would have cried the moment she heard my voice. Instead, tears fell only when she heard the news about Hazel. Yet even with this newfound realization, even with the knowledge that she had kept huge secrets from me regarding Hazel's life, I still felt the need to comfort her. I still felt the need to try to save her from this misery. "Mark said she'll be fine," I said.

A few more sobs shuddered into the phone before Mom got ahold of herself and asked, "Will you have her call me?"

And in that instant, I wanted to yell into the phone and tell her that, yes, I was fine. That, no, she didn't need to worry about me. That, no, I wasn't coming back no matter how much she begged or pleaded. But she never asked. She never wondered. She never begged.

"I'll tell her," I said just before I hung up the phone and cried.

Chapter Eleven

I dodged around a few tourists and slipped into Up The Creek, a little clothing store with headless mannequins modeling swimsuits in the front window. Overhead speakers played an instrumental version of some familiar song I couldn't place, while the low ceiling and the tightly stacked racks of clothes gave a claustrophobic feel to the white-walled store. A few shoppers lingered in the back near the shoe section, while a woman in her early forties with stringy blond hair held up two dresses in a mirror near the front, switching between one and the other.

The clerk, a guy in his twenties with shoulder-length brown hair, gave me a quick grin before he returned to refolding a stack of men's collared shirts on a display. I scanned the clothes, moving past the shorts and swimsuits and into the children's section.

Even though I wasn't certain if I was going or not, I searched through the baby clothes, hoping to find something in there I could get for Hazel's baby. Maybe a little pink dress with ruffles. Maybe a package of sleepers. What about socks? Did babies need those?

After a few minutes, I had three tiny outfits draped

across my arm, a bundle of bibs with funny sayings on them, and a package of three-to-six-month sized socks. But even as I calculated whether or not I had enough items to constitute an appropriate gift from the soon-to-be aunt, it just didn't feel right. All the items I had picked out could have come from anyone; a neighbor, a co-worker, even the dentist could have chosen these things.

What I needed was something more personal. Something that announced I knew Hazel better than just someone who cleaned her teeth every six months, even if I hadn't seen her in three years.

Across the store, a dark haired individual bobbing in and out of the racks near the hunting section caught my eye. I watched him for a second, huffing when the mystery shopper turned out to be Riley.

I didn't want a confrontation. I didn't want to talk to him. I didn't even want him to know I was in the same store as he was. So I stepped behind a display of little girls' hair bows, plastic necklaces, and tiny accessories, watching him as he walked to the front with a camouflage hat and shirt tucked beneath his arm. Cautiously, he scanned the store, his eyes flitting past my hiding spot and on to the woman in the shoe section when I remained motionless. As he took another quick glance around, I saw the new bruise he was sporting on his left eye and the angry gash on his busted chin.

"What happened to you, man?" the clerk asked when Riley set his things on the counter.

Riley lowered his head like he was trying to block the clerk's view and mumbled, "Nothing."

"That doesn't look like nothing," the clerk continued. "At least tell me you got some good ones in on the other guy."

Riley didn't say anything else as the clerk rang him up. When the clerk handed him his receipt, Riley yanked the bag from the counter and marched toward the front door. As he pushed outside, I made a move to emerge from my hiding place, but the hanger from the little pink dress I carried got hooked on the display, almost pulling it down on top of me. Everything started to crash around me, banging on the floor. Without a thought, I dropped the clothes and held the display with my hands, finally pushing it back in place. I cringed, certain that Riley must have heard the commotion and stopped. But when I looked back at the door, I was relieved to see that Riley was gone.

I picked up the scattered bows and jewelry, coming across a necklace that had a silver cross similar to the one that was still missing from my dreamcatcher. And in the next breath, I knew what I'd get for Hazel's baby: a dreamcatcher of her own. Putting the other items back, I headed to the checkout.

The clerk wasn't as talkative as he'd been with Riley. Maybe because I didn't have a big black eye or a busted jaw. But whatever the reason, it was fine with me and I was out of there quickly and on my way back to my car.

The sun beat down as I stepped from the shade of the storefront and toward the parking lot, but my hurried pace immediately slowed when I saw Riley leaning against the trunk of my car.

He propped his muddy boot on the bumper, crossed

his arms, and asked, "Spying on me?"

"Get off my car," I scoffed. "And take a shower. You're filthy."

"I heard you've been talking to Bill Dickerson," Riley said, ignoring my request.

I turned my attention to my bag as I dug for my keys. "That's none of your business."

"I'm making it my business," Riley said, pushing from my car and grabbing my arm. "What did he tell you?"

I shrugged free. "I thought you said he was crazy," I said. "So why worry about what he told me?"

"You didn't answer my question," Riley said as the little muscles in his jaw flexed.

"I don't have to." I pushed past him. "You aren't in charge around here. And even if you were, I'm not doing anything wrong."

"Yes, you are."

"Like what?" I scoffed. "Paying attention? Asking questions?"

"About things that don't concern you."

"Why does everyone keep saying that?"

Riley stepped closer. "Because it's true."

"I already told you, Riley, sooner or later, I'm gonna figure out what you have to do with all this."

"And then what?" Riley said, throwing up his hands. "What's your plan then?"

"I don't know," I confessed. "But it's not going to keep me from finding out."

A fire raged behind Riley's stare as he grabbed my upper arms and crowded me against the car. The heat from the sun-soaked metal scorched my back. "I'm not going to tell you again, Scarlett. Stay out of this," he seethed as his fingertips dug into my skin.

"Leave me alone, Riley," I said, my voice not at all as menacing as I intended it to be.

Riley leaned in closer and the pain in my arms pulsed. "Not until-"

I jerked my knee into his groin, ending his sentence and gaining my freedom. As he doubled over, I pushed him backward and to the ground and jumped into my car, locking the door as he got back to his feet.

Riley's necklace clinked against the glass as he lurched at my door. He banged on the window and his face twisted with anger and pain. "Scarlett," he said, his voice muffled, but the intensity coming through loud and clear.

I only had one more thing to say to Riley Shelton as I started my car. "YOU'RE. A. CREEP!" I yelled, then yanked the car in gear and sped away.

༺༻

A fresh round of Townies trickled into Lost Creek. I could spot most of the new ones strictly by the stark contrast of white skin against a blistering red from their all day excursions on the lake without any thought given to sun protection.

The sun was fading, and out on the deck, laughter trickled in the air like ribbons on the wind, fading and then growing louder as stories of the day's adventures came to light. I kept a sharp eye on the boardwalk, watching for

Riley, wondering what I would do if he showed up.

"Ma'am," a woman with black hair pulled back in a ponytail said as she pointed to her hamburger, "I ordered this medium-well with no onions."

"I'm so sorry," I said, taking the plate. "I'll have the kitchen cook you another one."

She huffed, clearly agitated. "Make sure they get it right this time."

I nodded and hurried through the side door, sliding the plate across the elevated bar to Mel. "Another burger, but medium-well, no onions this time," I said.

"That's the third order you've gotten wrong today," Mel noted.

"I know," I said. "I'm sorry."

He dumped the old burger in the trash. "Where's your head tonight?"

"I don't know," I lied with a shrug.

"Boy troubles?"

I chuckled, figuring that was an easy guess. "Not the kind of boy troubles you're thinking of."

"It's not with that guy Riley, is it?"

I couldn't stop my face from twisting in disgust. "No," I lied again. "And why would you even say that?"

Mel nodded behind me. "'Cause he's been over in that booth watching you walk in and out for the last hour."

Spinning around, I scanned the patrons' faces. But when I came across Riley's, his head was down and his attention was in a menu. I turned back to Mel. "He isn't even looking at me," I said, trying to hide the pure outrage that raced through me for not seeing him before now.

Mel quirked his brow and slid a burger across to me. "Trust me," he said, "he's been watching. And it's not just tonight either. He always stares at you when he's in here." He reached for something to his left, disappearing from the small window for a second. He returned wearing an amused grin. "I'm pretty sure Miss Priss has noticed it too."

"Fantastic," I said, huffing as I picked onions off the burger and slapped them on the counter in front of Mel. "No onions, remember?"

As I pushed out the door to the deck, I wondered if Rachel knew Riley was inside, hiding. Or if she thought he stared at me too whenever he was here. But it was hard to read what she might know or think between the daggers of hate she glared in my direction every few minutes.

"Here you go, ma'am," I said, sliding the corrected burger in front of the woman with black hair. "Is there anything else I can get you?"

"Some more sweet tea would be nice," she snapped.

I forced a flat smile, then went back inside, noting Riley's eyes dart to the table when I entered. What was wrong with him? What did he really think I was going to find out at work? Did he think I was going to conduct a background check on him or something when I had a lull in my shift? Did he think I was suddenly going to put two and two together about his connection to the demon and he wanted to be here to stop me before I blurted it out?

Before I pushed through the door, Mel caught my attention and wiggled his brow, pointing out he'd been right about Riley. I rolled my eyes and stepped outside.

After I deposited the drink with the woman, I checked on my other customers, passing out a few extra napkins to a table where the wind had carried theirs over the railing, refilling a few other drinks (each time noting Riley was still inside, watching), then cashing out two tables.

"Table for one?" I heard Rachel say as I checked on the woman with the black hair again.

When I turned, Bill Dickerson was settling in at a booth in my section. He glanced around nervously, just like he had on my first day.

"Haven't seen you in a while," I said, taking out my order pad. "How are you?"

"I'm okay" he said swiftly, his eyes darting from one side of the deck to the other. "You?"

I shrugged. "What can I say?"

"I heard your sister's in the hospital." His gaze held mine as he added, "What happened there?"

I swallowed back a lump in my throat as my eyes betrayed me. "Like I said, what can I say?"

Bill sighed, reaching for a menu as his shoulders slumped. "That's what I was afraid of."

"But she's doing okay," I said, trying to sound hopeful. "She should be home any day now."

"And then what?" Bill said.

As I looked into his tired eyes, I wanted to be able to tell him about Blake. I wanted to give him the same hope I held that something was being done - although I had no idea what - to find a way to stop the demon from hurting anyone else. But Blake's rules screamed in my head, leaving me with nothing to say except, "I don't know."

I got nervous when Rachel walked by, glancing at Bill. I could almost guarantee her next stop would be at Riley's table to tell him Bill and I were having a conversation. In a normal world, this wouldn't be such a big deal. But here, in Lost Creek, Riley was determined to keep us apart.

"Can I get you anything to drink?" I asked, tapping on my order pad, reverting to my duties as a waitress to hide evidence of our discussion.

"Some sweet tea," Bill said, twitching when a man at a table near the railing busted out in laughter.

"I'll be right back," I said, hurrying inside to check on Rachel's position. I gritted my teeth when I saw that I had been right.

I grabbed a glass and quickly filled it, hoping that, for some reason, if I could get the drink on Bill's table before Riley came waltzing out, demanding to know what we were talking about, that it would look less conspicuous.

But when I reached the deck, Bill's table was empty. I checked the boardwalk, hoping to catch a glimpse of him, but he was gone. The wind swept across the deck, ruffling a paper held down with a ketchup bottle in the middle of the Bill's abandoned table. When I picked it up, it was just a copy of an old newspaper clipping dated last summer.

I quickly shoved it in my pocket when the door burst open and banged against the wall. Riley marched out, scanning the benches, purposely keeping distance between us. "Where is he?" Riley asked, first to me then to Rachel.

I ignored him and set the iced tea in front of the woman with the black hair, who gave a quick grin for the refill.

"He was right here," I heard Rachel tell Riley. "Wasn't he, Scarlett?" she called out.

I turned around, my eyes wide with innocence. "Who?"

Rachel huffed. "You know exactly who I'm talking about."

I shrugged, then handed the table near the railing their check, as Riley hurried down the sidewalk. After being gone only a moment, he returned with a questioning glance at Rachel. When Riley walked back inside without so much as a word to me, I felt a bit triumphant.

"Thanks a lot, Scarlett," Rachel hissed as she turned to chase after Riley.

♔♔♕♕

After my shift, I headed to my car and shoved the tip money into my pocket, feeling the paper Bill had left for me still crammed in there. I pulled it out and read through the brief article.

MISSING HIKER FOUND

After three days in the woods, Michael Thompson of Dallas was found, dehydrated and sunburned, but otherwise safe, two miles from where he had started his hike alone on Saturday morning. Mr. Thompson claimed that he lost his way after a run-in with a strange, unexplainable animal in the area around Black Bear Falls. Local physician Dr. Brian Shelton stated that delirium can sometimes occur with extreme dehydration.

As I reread the article, I noted that, one, this had been going on since last summer, and two, Riley's dad had possibly started the cover-up even then, maybe pulling Sheriff Reed in when it got too large for him to handle alone. But the article didn't really tell me anything other than what I already knew, so I wondered what exactly Bill planned to do with it.

Maybe he was just giving it to me as some sort of outside proof that he wasn't crazy. That I wasn't crazy. But other than that, it was just another report that could be easily explained away.

"Have you missed me?" a voice said and I raised my head.

My heart banged against my chest when Blake stood there, leaning against my car, his biceps rigid as he crossed his arms, his eyes as bright and stunning as before, and his smile so magnificent I had trouble remembering how to breathe.

"Where have you been?" I said, quickening my pace. "Are you okay?"

"I'm fine," he said. "I was just worried when you weren't home."

I hated that my cheeks flushed from the way he looked at me. "I'm okay," I said, fumbling. "Really."

Blake pushed from the car, his expression solemn. "Nothing else has happened, has it?"

"Well, I haven't seen it again, if that's what you mean," I said, checking the parking lot.

Blake's brow creased as he tilted his head. "What are you not telling me, Scarlett?" He looked around like there would suddenly be some big clue in the middle of the parking lot that would reveal what I was hiding. "What's happened while I was gone?"

"I have this," I said, handing over the copy of the article Bill left for me.

"Where did you get this?" Blake asked, leaning in so close that I would have easily been able to identify what kind of soap he used, had I been able to form a coherent thought..

"Bill Dickerson gave it to me," I said. "He's seen it too." I pushed out a long breath to steady my shaking nerves. "He's the one who told me what it really was."

"When did he tell you all that?"

I blinked up at Blake, wondering why his tone had shifted. "Uh, right before everything happened in the kitchen."

"I specifically told you that you couldn't tell anyone about this," Blake said.

"You didn't tell me that until *after* I talked to Bill."

"But you're just now telling me that he knows?"

I shrugged. "I didn't think that mattered."

"Of course, it matters, Scarlett," Blake said, sighing. "I've trusted you with the secret of what I really am, and you purposely withheld information from me? Do you realize how much danger you could put me in?"

"I'm sorry," I said, reaching for Blake as tears pricked at my eyes. "He knew before I did, so I really didn't think it mattered."

Blake let the distance between us linger, then turned and paced the length of my car, running his hand through his hair as he walked. When he returned there was anger in his gaze. "Is there anything else?" he demanded. "Anything you're not telling me? Even the tiniest detail?"

"Well, there's Sheriff Reed and Riley Shelton."

"Who are they?" Blake asked slowly as his jaw clenched with frustration.

"Sheriff Reed's, well, he's the sheriff."

"I got that much," Blake said, waiting for more.

"And Riley's Dr. Shelton's son. The one in the article I gave you."

Blake shook his head. "But what do they have to do with all this?"

"They know about the demon."

Blake's eyes widened. "Both of them?" Blake asked. "Are you sure?"

"I'm pretty sure. I mean, they haven't just come right out with a sign announcing it or anything, but they're real worried about what I know."

Blake's voice lowered to a grumble when he asked, "What did you tell them?"

"I didn't tell him anything. I swear."

"Are you sure you didn't say one word? Anything about me? Anything about the demon in the kitchen?"

"No," I said, lowering my head. "Riley even pushed me against the car today, trying to get me to say something. But I didn't. I didn't say anything."

"Wait," Blake said. "Did you say he pushed you?"

I crossed my arms and nodded. Blake froze suddenly

when the sleeves of my T-shirt brushed up my arms, exposing the bruises left behind where Riley had grabbed me.

A fierceness welled up in Blake as his eyes held mine. And for the first time, I could see small streams of yellowish-gold expand from the pupil like solar flares, making me feel like I was staring into the sun, about to be blinded, but unable to look away.

"If I ever see Riley Shelton," Blake said coldly, "I'm going to kill him."

Chapter Twelve

Blake barely spoke to me as he walked me to the boathouse. I clung to the small bag holding the silver cross for the dreamcatcher, grasping it as tightly as I wanted to grab Blake's hand that, although I didn't know for sure, felt like he purposely withheld. I couldn't tell if he was more enraged at me or at Riley, or if it was a combination of the two. But either way, I didn't ask him about it. Something inside me couldn't handle the thought of him holding a grudge against anything I'd done - intentional or not. So I decided I would just believe it was his anger toward Riley that kept him silent.

That night when I turned out the lights and climbed into bed, I could see Blake out the front window on the deck, standing guard, his back toward me, his eyes on the dark forest. Even if he was furious with what I'd done, he was still there, watching over me.

When I woke up, the skies were gloomy and Blake was gone. And for most of the day, I mindlessly tinkered with the fragments of the dreamcatcher, putting the pieces back in their original places, but on a grapevine wreath instead. I had stared at the version Hazel had made every night for years and had memorized exactly where each Lego fit, how the ribbon from Mom's shirt twisted more on top of the wreath than on the bottom, and how one side of the bow made from Dad's tie was larger than the other. I took out the cross from the bag and put it in its place next to the Hello Kitty head. But even with it all back together, the dragonfly was still missing and the dreamcatcher was still incomplete.

I got up from the table, leaving it there to check out the window one last, fruitless time. Then I got ready and headed to my shift at The Spot.

A light rain fell on Lost Creek and thunder grumbled in the gray skies. A few moments after I arrived at The Spot, the lights flickered overhead, paralyzing us all for a moment as the unsteady electricity threatened to leave the restaurant in darkness. But when the steady glow returned, the conversation trickled out into the air again and everyone went back to what they were doing as if they'd never paused in the first place.

I leaned against the counter, watching time tick away on the clock on the far wall as I listened to Mel through the small window work at filling the lunch order for my table in the back. It had been almost twelve hours since I'd seen Blake last and the reason for his sudden disappearance worried me. Had his anger gotten the best of him and he just left, leaving me to figure all of this out on my own? Or had something happened, something wicked and evil, that forced him to leave his post outside of the boathouse?

Both scenarios were almost too much to bear.

Rachel hovered near Sheriff Reed's table, refilling his coffee every few minutes as he read the newspaper, lifting his gaze every so often to catch a glimpse of the customers coming in. I figured she was just keeping him as comfortable as she could for as long as she could, hoping Riley would show up after a while. I, on the other hand, could go another year without seeing him again.

A woman in her twenties rushed in out of the rain holding the hand of a young boy. She had a barrette holding her blonde hair out of her eyes, and the boy, I assumed to be her son, was a raggedy-haired six-year-old. Together they stomped their damp feet on the mat just inside the door, and as they headed through the diner, I could see the boy had more freckles than any kid I'd ever seen.

"Now, Justin," the woman said as he bounced on the bench seat in the booth, "this is not a playground. Sit down."

"What can I get you to drink?" I asked, pulling a pen from behind my ear as Justin plopped down in the seat, pouting and crossing his arms.

"Some chocolate milk," he said, glaring across the table at his mom.

"And what about you?" I asked the woman.

"A coffee."

I stopped by one of my other tables, checking if they needed any refills and letting them know their order would be up soon. Then I stepped into the kitchen and pulled a single-serve carton of chocolate milk from the cooler. When I returned, Rachel stood staring at the front door with a stupid grin on her face. For a moment, I didn't understand why. But when I turned toward the door I spotted Riley walking in.

It came so naturally, the glare that swept across my face. And I wanted more than anything to walk up to Riley and pour this chocolate milk over his head, getting some small payback for the bruises on my arms. But that would probably just get me fired. I looked back at Sheriff Reed watching me, and added arrested to that list.

A tiny fist gripped my shirt. "Give me my milk," Justin demanded, jerking me back to my responsibilities as a waitress.

"Oh, sorry," I said, handing it to him and pouring his mom her coffee.

As I slid their order across to Mel, my attention kept shifting to Riley, who still lurked near the front of the building with his muddled hair, and his clothes soaked through and caked with mud. Served him right.

"Hey, what do you think you're doing?" Jenny demanded, coming around the counter and pointing to the puddles of dirty water Riley was leaving on the floor.

Riley paused just long enough to register what Jenny was complaining about before he continued into the cafe, not caring even the slightest bit what kind of a mess he left in his wake.

"Hey, Riley," Rachel cooed.

Riley didn't bother to answer as he slid in across from Sheriff Reed, who had folded the newspaper and put it to the side.

"What can I get you to drink?" Rachel sang as she wasted another perfect smile on Riley.

"Coffee," he said flatly.

Rachel poured Riley's coffee, keeping a sharp eye on him as he stared into the blackness of the cup. "And what about you, Sheriff Reed? You doing all right?"

"I think we're good," Sheriff Reed said, then raised his eyebrows at Riley when Rachel turned to leave.

Riley answered his silent question with a lazy shrug and then dropped his head to study the menu.

"Order up," Mel said and dinged the bell behind me, startling me, just as Justin's mom signaled for a coffee refill.

To avoid a second trip, I balanced the first table's order in each hand, then I gripped the coffee pot with three free fingers. I was only a few feet away from depositing the food to the awaiting table when two small arms wrapped themselves around my legs, pinning me to a sudden standstill.

The plates hovered in place, defying gravity for a millisecond, before it took hold and yanked them to the floor, shattering them and sending food scattering across the tile. I stood there, frozen, as a hush fell across the entire cafe, every eye turning toward me, waiting on my next move. Then, as if completely unaware of any wrong doing, Justin squeezed my legs even harder, like he was afraid I would forget he was there.

"Justin," his mom called out, prying him from me. She quickly added, "I'm so sorry," as I walked away to the back room.

With a huff, I yanked the broom and dustpan from their resting place behind the back-room's door, wanting to march back to the table and shove them into Justin's little hands to make him clean up the mess he'd made. But when I returned, Justin sat on his knees, his hands folded neatly in his lap, his eyes wide as he looked down at the spread of food on the floor.

"I'm sorry," he said with the rasp of an approaching cry.

"It's fine," I said, feeling like I had the word SUCKER scribbled across my forehead as I swept up the mess.

"Need some help?" I heard someone say.

When I turned, Blake stood in the aisle, a stray piece of bread at his feet and a rueful smile on his lips.

I couldn't stop the large gasp that burst from my mouth, like some love-struck schoolgirl, as I dropped the broom. "You're okay," I whispered.

I could have stood there for an hour, soaking in the sight of Blake, but when Marcus, the busboy from the back, came out and picked up the broom to finish cleaning up the mess, I snapped back to reality and remembered where I was.

Every eye was on me - again - as I tried and failed to make this situation less awkward, "Can I get you some coffee or something?" I asked Blake like he was just some random customer.

"Coffee would be good," he said, taking an empty booth near the kitchen.

As I filled his cup, Mel signaled that the replacement orders were up, forcing me to leave Blake without getting a single answer about where he'd gone last night or if he had finally forgiven me for my shortcomings. It was nearly impossible not to just toss the plates on the designated tables and return to Blake. But when I saw the way Sheriff Reed and Riley were watching him stir a packet of sugar into his coffee, I had a feeling this situation was almost as treacherous for Blake as the forest was.

I made my rounds to the other tables, smiling and refilling drinks, before sauntering back to Blake. As I paused, pretending to refill his cup, I wondered what would happen if I pointed Riley out to Blake. Would he confront him? Would he demand that Riley keep his hands off me? But as I thought back to the gleam in Blake's eye last night, I had a feeling that what could have easily been taking as just a cliché remark about killing him might very well have be an actual truth.

"It might be time for you to go," I whispered to Blake, trying to hide the concern from my face. "Rule number two."

My breath caught in my chest when Blake's eyes met mine and a grateful smile stretched across his face. I had spent so much time wondering if he was okay. Wondering if I would ever see him again. And now that he was here with me, I had to send him away to ensure I wouldn't have to worry about that again.

Blake took the hint and slid from the booth. "Thanks for the coffee," he said, pulling out a twenty and laying it on the table.

As Blake headed to the front, Sheriff Reed and Riley quickly waved to Rachel for their check. She hurried to bring it to them with a big smile, but they just slapped their money on the table and took off, all but running to the front. I hurried after them, my heart pounding at the thought of them catching up with Blake. What would they do? Would they sense what he really was and take him away?

But as I reached the door, pressing my hands against the cool glass to get a better view of the situation outside, I was relieved when all I saw was Sheriff Reed and Riley searching an empty parking lot, and Blake nowhere to be found.

"Who was that?" Jenny said from behind the cash register, her eyes dreamy.

Rule number two, I reminded myself. "I don't know."

☙☙☙❧❧

A light drizzle still hung in the air when I hurried out to my car, but I slowed my walk when Riley was leaned against the back of it again. His hair and clothes were dark from dampness.

"Are we seriously doing this again?" I yelled. "Get off my car."

He kicked himself away and spun his keys in his hand. "Where you headed?" he asked.

I didn't answer since I knew Riley was just trying to find a reason to ask about Blake. Sheriff Reed had tried that earlier, after Blake's disappearance, by coming back in and telling me that because he was sheriff, it was his job to know everyone in this town. It was also his job to protect them, but he had conveniently forgotten that part, so I didn't feel so bad lying about not knowing a thing.

"Hey," Riley said, habitually reaching for my arm, then stopping himself before he took hold, "I'm talking to you."

"And I'm ignoring you," I said. "I don't have to tell you where I'm going."

"You're right," Riley said with a smirk. "Just like I don't have to tell you I'll just follow you and find out that way."

I gritted my teeth to the point where I thought they would crack. "Fine, if you must know," I seethed as I lied, "I'm going to visit Hazel."

There was twinge of disappointment in Riley, giving me a small surge of satisfaction. But then he said, "I'm headed there myself to see my dad," and all my triumphant joy drained away.

I got in my car and drove the short distance to the hospital with Riley behind me like a warden guarding his prisoner - cautiously, but almost daring me to change course and supply him reason to give chase.

Why did it matter, really, what I was doing? Didn't he have the rest of the town to inflict with this warped sense of entitlement? Why was he picking on me? On Blake?

To them, Blake was just a nameless face, and in a touristy town like Lost Creek, he wasn't the only one. So why worry about him? What had they noticed in that short amount of time he was in The Spot that caused them this kind of worry?

Without being any closer to figuring any of it out, I pulled into the hospital parking lot and got out to head inside, not bothering to wait for Riley. With his persistent claim of innocence about any responsibility of anything going on in this town and my refusal to give him one sliver of information about anything else I knew, I really didn't think we would have much to talk about on our way inside.

But even though I was a few steps ahead of him in the hospital, Riley shadowed me, turning down the same hallways, cutting up the same stairwells, even pausing when I stopped for a drink from the water fountain. It wasn't until I placed my hand on Hazel's door and pushed it open, that Riley finally turned to, supposedly, find his dad.

Inside the room, Hazel was asleep and Mark was sitting in a chair next to the bed, looking quite uncomfortable. He looked up from his magazine, then silently stole across the room, herding me back into the hallway.

"She just fell asleep," Mark whispered with a twitch in his expression that screamed he was holding something back.

"Is she still okay?" I asked.

It was as if my question knocked Mark in the gut and he leaned against the wall and ran his hand over his stubbly chin. "Dr. Shelton can't figure out why she's still having contractions."

I'd seen enough movies and heard enough about babies to know that pregnancy and contractions were in some sort of partnership. "But that's supposed to happen, right?"

"Yes, but not this soon," Mark said, the circles beneath his eyes darker than I remembered.

And for a moment, I wanted to save Mark from this torment, like I had tried to do with Mom when she'd learned about Hazel. But as he leaned, pressing his shoulder against the wall, there was an uncommon strength behind his anguish. Then, right there, in the middle of the hospital hallway, I finally saw my brother-in-law. I finally saw the man Hazel married. A man who would sit endless hours next to her bed, refusing to leave her side. A man who stood guard over her when she was at her weakest, while he carried the weight of worry and clung to threads of hope.

"But Hazel and the baby will be okay, right?" I asked again, needing hard reassurance.

"Yeah," Mark said, his voice raspy. "She just needs her rest."

I took the hint and pulled my keys from my pocket. "Well, I guess I'll head back," I said. "Will you at least tell her I came by?"

"Oh, wait," Mark said, holding up his hand to stop me. "Stay here. I'll be right back."

Before I could ask what it was about, Mark had already slipped quietly back into Hazel's room, leaving me in the hallway, standing alone.

At the end of the hall, a nurse passed, looking at me quizzically for a moment before disappearing around the other corner. I stepped toward Hazel's room, peering around the doorframe to see Mark, then fought back a slight shriek when he rushed out, almost colliding with me since I was closer than he had left me.

"I got you something," he said, handing me a white plastic bag. "Well, it's from both us. Me and Hazel."

My face scrunched with embarrassment and skepticism as I opened the bag and peeked inside, spotting two rolls of film. I raised my gaze to his and squinted, wondering if this was some kind of cruel joke. But when a smile slowly spread across Mark's face, I could see that he wasn't trying to mean about it.

"We got you two, in case you lose one of them," he said with a sheepish grin, trying to make light of the other night.

I really didn't think it was funny. But I knew he was trying. So I closed the bag back up and gave a quick grin. "Thanks."

I expected Mark to just nod and go back into the room, letting me head to the yellow house alone, but what I didn't anticipate was for him to wrap me in a hug. "Thanks for coming to check on her, Scarlett," he said before releasing me. "It means it a lot to her to have you here."

Falling back a step, I felt a twinge of guilt of using Hazel as a ruse to throw Riley off the trail of where I had really wanted to go earlier tonight: to see Blake. And with this newfound sense of regret, I thought about just handing him back the bag and turning to leave. But something kept me there, still and silent, waiting on Mark to elaborate and give me enough evidence for me to believe that Hazel wanted me around.

But after an awkward silence filled the bright hallway, Mark told me he would let Hazel know I had been there, then retreated back into the room. I pushed out a loud sigh, then hurried down the hallway with no other option but to cling to the same threads of hope Mark held on to.

Saving Scarlett

Chapter Thirteen

When I reached the parking lot, Riley's Jeep was gone and the rain had stopped. The night felt full of possibilities, full of hope. But after the short trek back to Bear Paw Lane, everything crashed around me again when I saw a sheriff's cruiser sitting in my parking spot in front of the yellow house.

I wondered if Riley had called Sheriff Reed after he had a visual that I was, indeed, at the hospital, giving them ample time to search the property for clues on what I knew. Clues about the mysterious guy in the cafe.

Slamming my car door, I marched to the cruiser, expecting to see Sheriff Reed sitting there, his mustache concealing his lips, his stare flat. But instead, Sheriff Reed had roped in some new help, a thirty-something deputy sheriff with thinning hair and a potbelly. He climbed from his car, the radio static humming in the background, and eyed me over.

He was doing all he could to be as intimidating as Sheriff Reed, but he was no taller than I was, and his wheezing from the small effort of exiting the vehicle gave me the impression that I could probably outrun him without even trying.

"What's your business here?" he asked, shining a flashlight in my face, blinding me temporarily before moving his attention to my car.

"I live here," I said, shielding my eyes. The light reflected off his badge, letting me know his name was Watson. "Is there some kind of problem?"

He returned his flashlight to the holder on his utility-belt. "Have you seen anything out of the ordinary? Anything, or anyone, you'd like us to check in on?"

He meant Blake.

"No," I said as evenly as I could. "But maybe if I knew what you were looking for, I could be more helpful."

"That's not any of your concern," Deputy Watson said, taking a quote from Sheriff Reed's *How to Run a Corrupt Town and Get Away With It* handbook.

"But you're sitting in front of where I live," I explained. "I'm pretty sure it concerns me, at least a little."

Deputy Watson squared his shoulders and cleared his throat, checking the shadows and ignoring my response.

"Can you, at least, tell me how long you plan on being out here, dealing with stuff that's not my concern?"

"For as long as it takes," he said. "Now, I think it'd be best if you just get on inside and let me do my job."

That night I sat, looking out the front window at Deputy Watson's cruiser parked in plain sight of the boathouse, knowing Blake wouldn't show. How could he?

Not with Sheriff Reed and Riley, in addition to their new helper, Deputy Watson, snooping around, just waiting for Blake to reappear so they could snatch him up and take him in for questioning on the grounds of being a stranger in a small town.

☙☙❧❧

The next day, I slept in, waking with just enough time to get to work. As I rushed to my car, glaring at Deputy Watson still *doing his job*, Kiki, in her perfect clothes and blond ringlets, ambushed me, her red Saab still humming as she blocked my retreat.

"Can I talk to you for a minute?" she said, climbing from her vehicle.

"I'm kind of in a hurry," I said, then shut my door.

This didn't deter her in the slightest and she tapped on the glass with her hot pink fingernail until I rolled it down. "Like I said, it'll only take a minute."

"Fine," I said, staring up at her. "What is it?"

"I haven't received your RSVP yet."

"You know there are far more important things going on in this town than a stupid baby shower, right?" I scoffed. "I mean, there's a sheriff's cruiser parked out here. Does that not set off any bells with you, even a little?"

I started to roll up the window and just run her over if she didn't move, but then decided against it when Deputy Watson stepped out.

Kiki smiled at him. "I think it's nice that the sheriff's department is able to watch over Hazel's house while she's in the hospital. Not many towns can say that."

"No, ma'am," Deputy Watson said, adjusting his utility belt. "Not many, indeed."

I was going to be sick, since I was pretty sure if Deputy Watson had had a hat, he would have tipped it at her.

"Look," I said, sticking my head out the window. "Can one of you please move your vehicle? I need to get to work."

"Not until you give me your RSVP," Kiki said as her smile faded. "If you just give it to me now, I won't have to bother you again."

A long second passed, both of us unwavering. But then I caught a glint of something in Kiki's eyes that made me realize she had much more time and energy to hound me about this day after day, until I finally gave in.

"Fine," I said with a huff. "I'll be there."

A flawless smile expanded across her porcelain face as she hurried back to her car. "Great," she said, stretching to see me from over the top of her car. "I'll put you down as attending. Do you have a plus one?"

"To a baby shower? No," I said, revving the engine. "Now, move."

The Spot had transformed into a festival atmosphere for Movies in the Moonlight, with music blaring an upbeat song and strings of lights running from the back of the deck, overhead to the grassy shores of Lost Creek Lake. A section of the parking lot was roped off and a ginormous grill sat behind a makeshift counter, with the scent of fresh hamburgers filling the air.

There were still a couple of hours before the movie started, but people were already showing up in droves, with blankets in hand, claiming their section of shore like a repeat of The Great California Land Rush. The busboys, Mike and Marcus, donned bright orange vests and waved flashlights near the street, directing cars to park down the road and away from the already full lot.

I was volun-told, along with another new waitress, Charlotte, to assemble the plain burgers and then put chips on the plate. Not exactly supplying-clean-water-to-a-third-world-country kind of work. But even so, it felt rewarding when Jenny glanced back from the cash register with a slight grin at Charlotte and me as we fell into a rhythm, sliding order after order across the side pickup table, getting people out of line and back to their awaiting blankets.

The sun was just melting into the trees when Jenny signaled Rachel to take her spot at the cash register. The line for hamburgers had dwindled to just a few last minute stragglers as Jenny headed across the lawn, zigzagging through the crowd to reach the screen. She looked so tiny standing in front of the towering white rectangle, waving her hands in the air to gain everyone's attention.

"Good evening," she yelled, but from this distance, it sounded muffled and small.

I found myself leaning in, turning my head, trying to hear her better as she continued to make announcements and introduce the movie. But the crowd grew anxious and a few guys threw out catcalls, starting a chain reaction of noise. Then all at once, the audience fell into applause and cheers, drowning out Jenny's voice. Even from across the way, I could see the embarrassed grin stretch across Jenny's face as she finally gave up and signaled for the movie start.

The screen burst into a bright white and the audience fell quiet with an occasional shush sounding from somewhere to the left.

Jenny returned, her face bright red, her eyes wide. "I hate getting up in front of everyone," she said with a loud sigh as she grabbed a bottled water.

The sun had finally set and the sky was dark as Mel lowered the flame on the grill and sat down on a stool a few feet away. Rachel and a few other girls gathered and started talking quietly amongst themselves, while Charlotte and Jenny seemed to mirror each other, standing just behind the counter, their arms crossed and their gazes fixed on the big screen. I grabbed a water bottle, stepped just outside the prep area and leaned against a tree, losing myself in the plot of the movie.

Every few minutes, I would check Jenny and the others, making sure I wasn't needed before coming back to the movie. Just as a car chase scene started, I felt my tether to Blake tighten, and I snapped from the movie, glancing around, wondering if he was here.

But as I gazed out over the sea of people blanketed in darkness, searching, the connection broke and a sudden wave of worry washed over me. What just happened? Why couldn't I feel Blake anymore?

"Enjoying the movie?" I heard from somewhere behind me.

When I turned, Riley stood there, snacking on a handful of chips, covered in a layer of dirt from his shoulders to his boots. The bruise beneath his eye was just a shade of light yellow now and the cut on his chin had healed completely.

I stared at Riley, trying to calculate how long ago I'd seen his fresh wounds, then recalculating when I kept coming up that it only yesterday. Riley just tossed another handful of chips into his mouth, crunching as he held my gaze.

"How're you enjoying that guard detail outside your house?"

"I love it," I said flatly. "Your idea?"

A smirk pulled at the edge of Riley's mouth, exposing a small dimple that I wanted to use as target practice.

"It's not gonna stop me, you know," I said.

Riley crunched another chip. "We'll see."

"Hey, Riley," Rachel called as she hurried over, touching his arm as soon as she was close enough. "You need a burger or something?"

"No," he said, shooting her a quick glance before returning his attention to me. "I'm just here to watch."

Infuriated, I turned to Jenny. "I'm taking a break," I yelled, then walked away before she even acknowledged me.

I wasn't sure where I was going. All I knew was that I wanted to be somewhere other than where Riley was. Somewhere he couldn't see me. Somewhere he couldn't watch me. I had only made it a few feet when Riley caught up with me and blocked my path, once again changing his mind and forcing himself to drop his hands back to his side when he reached to grab me.

"Just leave me alone," I said, stepping around him.

Riley raced around me again, walking backwards, staying in my path. "Tell me where you're going."

"Somewhere you're not."

"Is there a problem?" a voice thick and harsh called from shadows, giving both Riley and me pause.

As we turned, Blake stepped forward, standing just at the edge of where the light faded into the black. But even in the murk, I could see the same anger that had burned in his eyes last night.

There was charge in the air and the tendons in Riley's neck grew taut and his chest rose with a heavy breath. Then in one swift movement, Riley pushed me back a step and stood between me and Blake.

"I wondered when you were going to show up," Riley snarled as his back muscles rippled beneath his shirt and his hands closed in on themselves.

Blake's eyes narrowed. "You need to leave Scarlett alone," he said in a tone that sounded more like a growl.

"I was about to say the same thing to you."

"But you heard her," Blake said with a quick twitch of his eyebrow. "She's asked you nicely."

"I think we both know that's not going to happen."

"Wait," I said, feeling like I was missing something huge. "Do you two know each other?"

"In one way or another," Blake smirked. He kept his eyes trained on Riley. "You're Riley Shelton, aren't you?"

"And what name are you going by these days?"

But instead of answering, Blake just punched Riley in face.

Chapter Fourteen

A scream filled the night air, and for a second, I thought it was mine. But then Rachel was suddenly there, still screaming, tending to Riley on the ground as blood seeped from the corner of his mouth. He got to his feet, shoving Rachel out of the way the same way he'd done to me a few moments before.

As he rushed toward Blake, I jumped between them, closing my eyes, holding my breath, hoping they would stop before they collided and crushed me. Then after a silent moment, I dared a peek, noting only an inch of barrier stood between us all.

Riley seemed taller than I remembered, towering over me, meeting Blake's glare face to face. But as I stood there, shielding Blake, a torment, a struggle landed in Riley's eyes when he momentarily gazed down at me, then fell back a step, surrendering his position.

In a rush, I turned to Blake, pounding on his heaving chest, trying to move him back and out of sight. "Come on," I said, but he stood there like a stone statue, unwavering and immobile.

The tether in me stretched, bringing with it a pain

so wretched, so strong, I was afraid it was trying to warn me that if Blake didn't leave at that exact moment, the connection would be lost and I would never see him again.

"Please," I pleaded again as the crowd started to come together around us. "You have to go," I whispered. "Remember rule number two."

Blake blinked back to the present and he stared down at me with the fire still raging in his eyes. "Remember every rule, Scarlett. Remember what I told you," he whispered in my ear. "I'm your only hope."

I tear raced down my cheek as Blake stepped into a thicket of trees and disappeared.

"What's going on here?" a man yelled from behind the sea of spectators. And as they parted, I quickly wiped away the tear when Sheriff Reed spilled out. His eyes widened as they moved between Riley and me. "I said, what's going on?" he yelled louder, making me jump.

"He's gone," Riley said flatly, feeling the wound at the side of his mouth with the tip of his tongue. "But it looks like our little Townie here has herself a boyfriend."

"Does she now?" Sheriff Reed said slowly as he turned toward me. "Well, this makes our job just a little bit easier, now doesn't it?"

He put his hand on my shoulder to guide me away from the crowd, but I shrugged it off.

"Am I under arrest for something?" I said, glaring at Sheriff Reed and Riley. "If anything, you should arrest Riley."

"For what?" Riley barked. "I'm the one that got punched in the face, remember?"

"Yeah," I said, "and you deserved it."

Riley let out long-suffering sigh, then clenched his jaw as he exchanged a knowing glance with Sheriff Reed.

"Neither of you are under arrest," Sheriff Reed clarified. "I just have a few questions for you. Figured we could head on down to the station. That is, unless you wanted everything aired out here."

When I turned, I felt like I was on the giant movie screen and every eye was on me, watching, wondering what was going to happen next.

I scowled at Riley, wishing more than anything that looks could kill, or at least cause insufferable pain, as he opened the back door of the sheriff's cruiser.

"Fine," I said and got in.

⋘⋘⋙⋙

I could say this was a first, being questioned in a sheriff's office. But in the last couple of weeks, I had had enough firsts - much more alarming than this - to last me until my mid-thirties. So the anxiety of what I should have been feeling was more like the inconvenience of a stuffy nose.

The sheriff's office smelled like a mixture of stale coffee and wet dog, making me long for a window I could crack open to air this place out. In addition, the desks and chairs looked like they'd been here since the 1970s, which looked like the last time they'd been cleaned as well.

"Have a seat," Sheriff Reed said, offering me a chair like I had stopped by for tea.

Sitting, I crossed my arms, feeling like the little boy Justin when I added a pout.

"Now tell us about this guy. How do you know him?"

I huffed when Riley took a seat against the wall and mindlessly started tinkering with the rings at the end of his necklace. "Does he really have to be in here for this?"

Sheriff Reed glanced back at Riley like it was no big deal, but he ignored my question. "I'm not gonna ask you again, young lady."

"Good, because I'm tired of hearing the question," I said to Riley instead of Sheriff Reed.

"It'll go a lot smoother if you just cooperate with us," Sheriff Reed said and I got the impression that he was trying to smile, but with his mustache in the way, I couldn't be sure.

"Look," I said, inspecting the empty desks around us, "don't I get a phone call or something?"

"Who'd you want to call?" Riley chimed up with a gleam in his eye.

I huffed. "Well, not *him*, obviously."

"So you do know him," Sheriff Reed said.

I remained silent.

Sheriff Reed leaned back in his chair. "The other day, you told me you didn't know who he was. Were you lying then or are you lying now?"

"Why don't you turn your chair around and start questioning your little wanna-be-mayor over there? He seemed to know who he was," I said, narrowing my eyes on Riley. "How is that?"

"That's not your concern," Riley added.

"Is that your answer for everything?"

"When it comes to this, yes."

As I shook my head, I spotted a file on Sheriff Reed's desk with my name on it. "And what's *this*?" I yelled as I grabbed it. "You seriously have a file on me? Are you crazy? That's got to be some sort of invasion of privacy or something."

Sheriff Reed reached for the file, but I jerked to my feet and stepped back, opening it up. There were a few pictures of me, of the boathouse, of Hazel, of Bill Dickerson. But before I could see anything else, Riley was suddenly in front of me, yanking it away.

"You people are insane," I yelled, watching Riley hand the file back to Sheriff Reed, who then locked it away in a drawer.

Riley opened his mouth, but I held up my hand to stop him from saying anything. "Let me guess," I said slowly. "This is not my concern."

"You're catching on," Riley said, putting distance between us as if he could hear all the terrible things I wanted to do to him.

"Well, here's a little something you can catch on to. I don't have to answer to you, Riley. And I don't have to answer to you," I said to Sheriff Reed, stuttering when I felt like I had crossed some huge line, and added, "unless I break some *real* law."

Before they could say anything else, the door opened and Mark stepped in, followed by Hazel. "What's going on?" he said. "We got a call from Jenny that Scarlett was arrested."

I wanted to disappear right there. "I didn't get arrested," I said, hating that Mark still looked at Sheriff Reed to see if I was telling the truth.

"No, no," Sheriff Reed said, his voice lighter than before. "There was just little squabble down at The Spot and we brought Scarlett in to answer a few questions about what she knew."

Hazel rubbed her belly and sighed. "Did you tell them everything?"

"I'm done here," I said, skating past her question.

For a moment, I thought Sheriff Reed and Riley would say something to stop me. But as I walked toward the door, I realized they couldn't say anything without either arresting me or telling me exactly what Riley had to do with all of this. The door shut behind us and I climbed in the car, knowing they wouldn't do either.

CBCBEOBO

I gave Hazel and Mark the short version of the story: Riley got into a fight and they thought I had something to do with it.

And although I did, I left that part out. I also left out the part of Blake being there, and all the other spiritual aspects that made the story so unbelievable that even I had a hard time accepting it as the truth.

When we pulled onto Bear Paw Lane, Deputy Watson was still sitting in his cruiser, reading a western novel, barely glancing up as we passed.

"That was very nice of Sheriff Reed to have him

watch our house like this," Mark commented as he parked.

From the backseat, I rolled my eyes and tried not to throw up in their car. As I stepped out, Mark pulled Hazel's bag from the trunk and I felt like such a jerk. I had been so caught up in everything going on tonight, between the fight and the sheriff's office, which I hadn't even realized when I saw Hazel walk through the door that she had been released from the hospital.

Suddenly, Hazel seemed so fragile and vulnerable out in the open. I herded her into the kitchen, putting myself between her and sharp corners, afraid that she would instantly impale herself on them or something. Mark seemed to have similar fears as he hurriedly pulled out a chair from the kitchen table and made Hazel sit and rest.

"I'm fine," Hazel said, eyeing us both. "Really."

"We know," Mark said, but he didn't back down. "Do you need anything?"

Hazel put her purse on the floor next to her and scooted her chair closer to the table. "I'd love some ice cream," she said, then turned to me. "You want to join me?"

I shook my head, all at once feeling like I was intruding on their lives. But before I got the chance to verbally say no, Mark handed me the scoop and a carton of ice cream, then set two bowls on the table.

"You keep her company," Mark said, "while I take her bags upstairs."

A strange apprehension washed over me as I stood in the kitchen, alone with my sister. Even though Mark's and Kiki's words replayed in my head that Hazel had wanted me around, it was different now that she was out of the hospital and off medication, watching me, possibly judging me, wondering why I was still there.

"Sit down," she said with a quick grin.

I sat across from her while she opened the ice cream, and if I squinted my eyes just so, she could almost pass as a younger version of Mom. A different version of Mom. The one I wished, and maybe Hazel too, had been around to raise us.

I wondered how different our lives would have been. Would Hazel still have left? Would *I* still have left? Each of us in search of a new life, but still bound together, still inevitably designed by some unseen plan to find each other again.

"You still like strawberry, right?" Hazel asked, knocking me from my thoughts as she handed me a bowl.

"Yeah," I said, doing all I could to keep the lump in my throat manageable.

I lowered my gaze, swirling the ice cream around with my spoon, trying to think of something, anything, to talk to Hazel about, other than the zillion things that were forbidden for me to mention.

"Are you ready?" I blurted, surprising us both. "I mean, to be...unpregnant?"

Hazel pressed her lips on either side of the spoon, pulling it out slowly as she scraped it clean, then let it linger in front of her. "Sometimes," she said, a ghost of a smile on her face. "Like now," she added with a slight laugh. "I just wonder what kind of Mom I'll be."

I knew it wasn't just a thought for her, but a fear. The

same fear I had about myself when eventually that time would come for me to be a mother. I mean, was there some sort of Mom-cell deficiency that we were not aware of, some trait we inherited from our mother that would hinder us from loving our children in a normal manner? In all fairness, we both knew, deep down, Mom loved us, just in her own, warped way. I think that's what scared us most of all - that there was love in the home we were raised in, but that it just never found its way to us.

"I think you'll be a great mom," I said.

Hazel seemed to suddenly solidify, her spoon at the edge of her open mouth, her eyes on me. At first, I wondered what was wrong, what I'd done. But then, slowly, she defrosted, blinking back the tears, her chin quivering. "Thank you, Scarlett."

Hazel cleared her throat as the room started to feel lighter. "And what about you?" she asked, dipping her spoon back into her bowl. "Are you ready?"

"For what?"

"To be an aunt."

I drew in a long, deep breath, then let it slowly seep out. "I guess," I said, not knowing what else to say.

Mark came back downstairs just as we finished the ice cream. "How long do you suppose that guy's gonna sit out there?" he said with a nod toward Deputy Watson parked on the street, bringing back the thoughts of everything that had happened tonight.

My guess would be Deputy Watson would eventually need to submit a change of address, since he wasn't going anywhere anytime soon.

I took our bowls to the sink and rinsed them out, wondering where Blake was, wondering if he was okay. But more than that, I wondered if I would see him again.

Blake's words replayed in my head: *Remember the rules. Remember what I told you. I'm your only hope.*

Now shaded in my memory, they seemed so desperate, so final. If he was my only hope, sent here to protect me, to protect Hazel, but couldn't get here because of the patrol camped out on the curb, because Sheriff Reed and Riley were doing all they could to keep him away, then what hope of survival did any of us really have?

Hazel yawned and headed up to bed. "I'll see you in the morning, Scarlett."

I swallowed hard, hoping she was right.

Chapter Fifteen

A week had passed with no sign of Blake. No tethering. Nothing.

I had hardly slept, making me about as pleasant and as good-natured as a dressed-up cat. Each night, I sat on the couch I'd pulled to the front window of the boathouse and looked out over the back lawn for any shadows I couldn't explain, listening for any screams from the yellow house. I wasn't sure what I would do if I saw or heard anything, but I didn't want to be taken by surprise.

Not again.

Kiki hadn't been much help with my mood either, as she found an excuse each day to come to the boathouse and examine the deck. Three different days she found the salt had returned. I argued with her every time that it wasn't me and that I had no idea where it came from, that all I knew was that sometimes it would be there when I woke up after a rare couple of hours of sleep, and sometimes it would be there when I got home late at night.

Kiki didn't believe me. But I didn't care and finally got tired of cleaning it up and just left the salt piled on the deck. The next time Kiki asked, I handed her a broom and told her if it bothered *her* so much, *she* could clean it. Coincidentally, that was the last time Kiki inspected the deck.

Mark and Hazel were getting a little weary of Deputy Watson's constant vigil. But Sheriff Reed assured them that it was for a neighborhood watch, not their house specifically, and that it just so happened that that particular spot was the best view of all the houses.

I knew it *was* a better view, but not of all the houses - just the boathouse.

Riley and Sheriff Reed were still stopping by The Spot, asking about Blake. Now I wasn't lying when I told them I didn't know where he was, but that didn't matter. They still thought I was withholding something. I had a feeling they wouldn't believe me no matter what I said.

Jenny was furious at me for the scene at last Friday night's Movies in the Moonlight, even though I told her that everything that had happened was completely out of my control. She finally forgave me - but just barely - when this Friday night's Movies in the Moonlight ended without a fight I was somehow connected to.

That evening, I pulled in behind Deputy Watson and gave a very sarcastic wave to him as I headed to the boathouse. It took him a moment, but eventually, he lowered the new western novel he was reading and waved back.

The yellow house was already dark, as Hazel and Mark had evidently turned in for the evening. As I walked the cobblestone path, something on the small retaining wall between the properties caught my eye. I stepped closer, glancing back at Deputy Watson to make sure his attention was still elsewhere, and picked it up.

I immediately saw that it was a *Find Yourself in Lost Creek* guidebook that had been tucked beneath a rock.

For a moment, I wondered what it was doing out here, who had left it. But when I flipped the guide over to the map on the back and saw a circle drawn around a road just north of here, my heart raced. Blake was still here.

I hurried back to the boathouse, constructing a plan to get out of here without Deputy Watson noticing.

Inside, I took my time heating and then eating a bowl of chicken noodle soup, passing by the front window every few minutes so Deputy Watson could catch a glimpse of me. I rinsed out the bowl and set it beside the sink, feigning a yawn, just in case his vision was extraordinary, then flicked off every light, including the one that shined out over the deck and part of the lawn closest to the lake.

I perched myself by the window, watching Deputy Watson from the shadows, and just as I expected, he climbed from his cruiser and brought his flashlight to life. His walk was slow and methodical as he moved around the yellow house, checking the bushes near the walls, investigating the back porch, examining the stairs to the boathouse, then shining the light in the large window, making me drop to the ground.

My breath caught in my chest as I gazed up at the beam of light still illuminating the window. Had he seen me? Was he on his way up here to tell me it was a town-security issue that I turn the porch light back on?

But then the window grew dark again and I dared a quick glance, just in time to spot Deputy Watson inspecting the chairs on the lawn, Mark's BBQ grill, then a wooden bench off to the side, as he headed back to his car.

It was almost two o'clock in the morning, three hours since I'd seen any significant movement from Deputy Watson. I had slipped on a pair of dark jeans and a black hoodie over a tank top, and now stood ready for my great escape.

One last check on Deputy Watson still in his cruiser, motionless, and I stepped outside, cringing when the small creak of the deck sounded more like an alarm after a bank robbery. I held my breath as I tiptoed down the stairs, then crept across the back lawn, using the yellow house as cover. When I reached the back porch, I pulled out the key Kiki had lent me and unlocked the door. Inside, I paused, listening for any signs that Mark or Hazel had heard something and were getting up to investigate. But after a moment of silence, I knew it was safe to proceed through the kitchen. The light from the front hallway gave enough illumination for me to find what I was looking for: Hazel's car keys.

In the garage, I disconnected the pull-chain on the automatic garage door opener, and then slid the door up, taking my time to lessen the sound. When I was done, my heart pounded in my chest as I readied to look around the corner at Deputy Watson, knowing this was going to either give me clearance or condemnation. I held my breath and leaned.

A shrub stood between us, forcing me to take another alarming step away from the sanctuary of the garage. As I peered around the bush, relief washed over me when I saw Deputy Watson's head tilted back and to the side, his mouth open, and his eyes closed.

I'm not technically stealing her car, I told myself, trying and failing to alleviate a sudden surge of guilt as I pulled from the driveway in Hazel's silver Mini Cooper, releasing a nervous breath I'd been holding when I passed Deputy Watson and he didn't even stir. I was just borrowing her car - without her permission - out of necessity, really. I couldn't drive around town in my white Taurus, since I was certain it was on some kind of A.P.B. at the sheriff's office as belonging to a "person of interest." Plus, if Deputy Watson woke up and found my car missing, he'd call Sheriff Reed, who would probably assemble the Army Reserve to search for me.

I headed to the place circled on the map: a bridge just to the north, where the creek the town was named after ran beneath the road. When I reached it, I pulled onto the shoulder, easing Hazel's car into the grass and onto a flat clearing that was hidden from passing vehicles.

I killed the engine and turned out the lights, making the world seem darker and more intimate, like nothing existed past the few feet I could see out the windshield. After a few moments, I wondered where Blake was.

Thirty minutes passed and the air inside the Mini turned muggy and I peeled off the hoodie, savoring the slight coolness, before it thickened up again. I opened the car door and stepped outside, feeling like I could breath once more as a breeze came at me cool and fresh. The creek babbled a few feet away and I ventured toward it, checking the openness around me every few feet, imagining Blake suddenly there, his smile bright enough to light up the darkness.

But then something occurred to me a bit belatedly: How long had that paper been there? A day? Two? A week?

What if Blake had left it last Friday after everything with Riley, then came out here to wait for me, but I never showed? Did he think I wanted nothing to do with him anymore and just moved on, forgetting his promises to me? Did he leave me here to face that thing alone?

The moon was just over the horizon, illuminating the tips of trees in the distance and casting a glow across the water that made it look like liquid silver as a knot grew in my gut, doubling me over. A wave of nausea washed over me, making me hot and then cold, when I thought of never seeing Blake again. In a frenzy, I wrapped my hair, that now seemed to cling to my clammy neck, into a bun on top of my head, then crouched next to the river, splashing my face.

My breath grew ragged as I stared down at the small pebbles in the creek, trying to figure out how I was going to find Blake. How was I going to let him know he was still my only hope?

Before I lost myself in misery, a splash sounded a few yards upstream and I got to my feet, my hands shaking, my eyes wide. A frigid breeze swept across me, pimpling my skin. I tried to tell myself that the wind hadn't changed, that it was just from the effect of the cold water on my flesh and the small bout of hysteria I was suddenly feeling. But then the sensation that I wasn't alone surrounded me.

A sudden rush of heat brushed against my back.

I spun around, finding the space behind me open. I

jerked my attention to the river, to the shadows, to the car, finding nothing.

Slowly, I backed away, feeling behind me for the car with one hand as my eyes darted this way and that way across the openness in front of me.

"Blake," I said, my voice trembling. "Is that you?"

But the silence just screamed back at me.

My hand, shaky and sweaty, found the solidity of the car and I pressed my back against it, shuffling down the side, gripping blindly for the door handle. But the moment my fingers slipped around it, the car beeped and the lights flashed as the door locked.

Incredulous, I faced the car and yanked on the handle, seeing the keys still in the ignition, not wanting to believe what was happening. Then everything within me stopped when a breath, warm and sulfuric, fell on my neck, sticking to my skin. From my periphery, I could see a darkness grow. A darkness that was deeper than the night. A darkness that was evil and wicked. A darkness that had been after me since I arrived in Lost Creek.

My mind was screaming for me to run, to cry out for help, to turn around and fight, to do something other than just stand there and be a victim. But every ounce of strength I thought I had vanished when the demon said my name.

In a breath, the black fog enfolded me, cinching my arms and legs to my body, while the demon wrapped his fist around my neck. I wiggled, gasping, as it lifted me from the ground and tossed me over the hood.

I rolled all the way across, banging my shoulders and

elbows against the metal, grasping for anything to stop me, before I slammed into the ground, spitting grass and dirt from my mouth. My hand automatically found my neck, trying to erase the pressure that was still there from the demon's grip moments before.

Coughing, disoriented, I pushed myself to my feet, staggering on the flat ground that now seemed tilted in some way. I could see the dark figure as it approached, and though my vision was fuzzy from trauma, it didn't matter if I could see the horrid details. I knew what it was and that I only had a few precious seconds left before the demon easily finished the job of killing me.

"Don't," I squeaked, holding up my hand to stop it as a tear raced down my cheek when I thought about Hazel. About Mark. About Blake.

Would they ever know what happened here?

I stumbled back another step, tripping and falling to the ground, and the beast pounced on top of me, snarling as its weight crushed my chest. I wheezed, flailing and clawing at the dirt, trying to find some traction to pull myself from beneath it, trying to find some sort of weapon. But my futile attempts stopped when the demon smirked and then plunged its claws through my right arm, stopping only when the ground gave resistance.

My skin sizzled and a scream lodged in my gut as I wrenched in pain, unable to cry as I was suffocating. As I was dying.

Please, God, I silently pleaded as I stared at my arm, blinking in disbelief at what I was seeing, blinking against the pain, wanting to wake up from this terrible nightmare.

Then the monster twisted his hand and snapped the bone, knocking me to the edge of losing consciousness.

"Look at me," it demanded, bringing me back with a voice that shook my body.

I knew I would make it furious, but squeezing my eyes shut was my only way to fight, my only way to defy it, my only way to extend what little time I had left.

"Open them," it said with its breath on my face and a line of saliva stinging as it raced down my cheek to my neck. "I want to see your eyes when you die."

A high-pitched whistle filled the air and I felt the beast sit up. I dared a quick peek and then watched as a comet-like light collided with the demon, knocking it off my chest. The muddled mass of light and darkness plowed into the earth, throwing dirt into the air and on me as I gasped for air, crying when I tried to move my arm.

The light continued to move, smacking into the demon, knocking it to the ground as it passed by, then circled back for another strike. Knowing I had to get out of there, I bit back the pain and got to my feet, just as the demon lurched through the sky and tangled with the light. They spun out of control, crashing to the ground, sliding through the creek, shooting into the sky, as spectacular bursts of light filled the darkness like a tornado engulfing transformers.

But the struggled shifted again, turning back toward me as I raced to the car. They smashed into the ground with a crack that rivaled thunder. I shielded myself as it rained dirt and rocks on top of the car and on top of me.

As I raised my head, the light separated itself, putting

distance between it and the demon, then grew in size and intensity, turning into a dazzling brilliance brighter than the sun. The demon shrunk in on itself, shifting to the dark vapor I'd seen in the corner of the kitchen, before it shot across the river toward the trees in the distance, with the light giving chase.

Breathless and broken, I stood next to the car, gaping at the destruction, gaping at the utter silence that was now surrounding me. My breath sawed from my chest as I turned back to the car, melting into tears when it was still locked.

Frustrated, I stepped back and looked for a rock to smash in the window, but then stopped when I spotted something on the hood. Slowly, I wiped back the tears and then blinked in disbelief as I pulled Riley's necklace from the debris.

Chapter Sixteen

My arm was heavy and useless, just hanging from my shoulder, aching. As blood seeped down my arm, dripping from my fingertips and onto the leather upholstery, I knew I should go to the hospital or at least call 9-1-1. But that would only guarantee Sheriff Reed would know my location. He'd know I was still alive and know right where to send Riley to finish the job.

So I drove Hazel's Mini down the road with one purpose in mind: find Bill Dickerson.

He was the only one in Lost Creek who would believe what really happened to me. He would be the only one to give me guidance on what I should do next. And I had a strong feeling he would be the next place Riley was headed.

I just needed to reach him before then.

As I slinked through the pre-dawn streets of town, hoping to spot Bill's blue pickup in front of some house or parked outside some storefront, I wondered what had sparked the attack tonight.

Riley had had numerous chances. Sheriff Reed and he had gotten me alone at the station. Why not do it then? Was it because there had been too many witnesses that saw me leave? Had Riley just been toying with me the last few weeks before finally growing tired of me snooping around? Had he thought I had suddenly become a viable threat? Or was he just getting rid of all the witnesses, afraid someone might believe our crazy stories?

A knot formed in my throat as I choked back tears, thinking of Bill. He would be just as surprised, caught off-guard just as much as I had been. But a speck of hope still remained when I thought I might have been the first on Riley's hit list and Blake had been able to capture Riley before he reached Bill.

The search of the roads proved to be fruitless and a new idea came to me. I raced the car through the streets, hoping I remembered the way.

I finally exhaled when I pulled into Jenny's driveway.

Her yellow Beetle was there, but the windows were dark. I banged on the door, breaking the silence and making a dog bark somewhere off in the distance. A light suddenly filled a small window at the top of her door.

"Who is it?" she asked, her voice muffled.

It took me a second before I blurted, "It's Scarlett."

Deadbolts clicked, then the door pulled back just enough that I could see Jenny's weary eye peek out. Then she blinked away the sleep, replacing it with shock when she swung the door open wider and stepped out onto the porch with me. "What happened to you?" she said, hesitating just before she touched me.

"Where does Bill Dickerson live?" I asked, my lip feeling like it was the size of an orange.

"Bill did this to you?" Jenny squawked.

"No," I said, shaking my head as the edges of everything turned fuzzy.

"Who did this?" Jenny asked again, this time grabbing my arm, sending a jolt of pain through me as I sucked in all the air around me. She dropped her hold. "Talk to me, Scarlett. What happened?"

My chest grew tight, making it feel like the demon was sitting on it again, robbing me of oxygen. I staggered a step and tried to focus on Jenny. "Where's Bill?" I said just before everything went dark.

ೞೞೞೞ

I'd been dreaming about Mom. About the day I left. The urge to flee rushing through me again, screaming for me to just run, as voices crowded in on me, then softened into a whisper that sounded like leaves rustling in the wind.

Slowly, I opened my eyes and blinked at the unfamiliar ceiling, the pictures of a smiling family that I didn't belong to, the dark scratchy couch I was lying on.

When I stirred, a voice from somewhere over my head said, "Just take it easy."

My chest heaved as I started to look for Blake, but then stopped when a dull pain shot through me.

"Try to stay still," Jenny said, coming in and out of focus.

"What's going on?" I said with heavy blinks. "What happened?"

"I didn't know what happened to you," she said, "so I called Sheriff Reed."

"What? No," I said, pushing past the pain and sitting up.

"It's okay, it's okay," Jenny said. "He sent Dr. Shelton to come help you."

My breath was suddenly rushing in and out of my nose. "Dr. Shelton?" I repeated. "Riley's dad?" I shook my head, reaching for Jenny. "No, no, no," I stuttered. You can't tell them I'm here. They'll-"

Dr. Shelton stepped from the kitchen, wiping his hands on a towel. "You should be fine," he said flatly.

"Where's Riley?" I said, suddenly feeling for the necklace, then releasing a breath when it was still around my neck, hidden under my tank top. "Is he here somewhere too?"

"No," Dr. Shelton said, his face remaining stern, "he's...out."

I got to my feet, struggling against the sling across my chest that I hadn't noticed until then.

"I have to get out of here," I said, grabbing Hazel's car keys from the coffee table before losing my balance. I held on to the wall, blinking back the dizziness.

Jenny easily snatched the keys from me. "You aren't driving anywhere, Scarlett."

"But I have to," I said as a tear raced down my cheek.

Jenny stood there, sizing me up. She finally huffed, "Fine, but I'll drive you."

Outside, the sun shone high in the sky, and I blinked back the brightness, trying and failing to shield it from my eyes.

"What time is it?" I asked Jenny.

"About two."

"In the afternoon?" I stuttered.

Jenny gave a quick nod and unlocked the Mini. A few moments ago, this seemed like a good idea, Jenny driving me to the yellow house and then Mark driving her back. Yet when I looked at Hazel's car and saw the dented hood, the missing window, and the shattered glass littering the seats and floorboard, gleaming in the sun, I suddenly wanted to reconsider.

But before I had time to come up with anything better, Jenny leaned over and opened up the passenger's side door. "Get in."

The engine roared as Jenny hurried back to town, cutting corners, slamming on the brakes and peeling out afterwards.

"You never told me what happened to you last night," Jenny said, glancing at me from the corner of her eye.

I thought about telling her everything - about Riley, about Blake, about the spiritual manner in which they somehow knew each other. But instead, I turned and stared out the window, running through the rules in my head, knowing she wouldn't believe me anyway.

Jenny turned on Main Street, skidding to a stop when the traffic was backed up from the bridge.

"What's going on up there?" Jenny said as the craned her neck to see around a white Volvo. "Come on, people," she yelled, laying on the horn, reminding me of Riley.

I suddenly felt nauseous and a wave of cold sweat washed over me, making little beads pop up on my forehead. Without thinking, I wiped them away with my right hand, then stopped. I knew I had seen the demon's claws pierce my flesh, I had felt and heard the bone crack, rendering it limp and useless. But now I could raise it with only a slight twinge of tenderness?

Slowly, I peeked beneath the sling, pulling back the gauze wrapped around my upper right arm, then stared in disbelief when the puncture wounds were already covered with red, new tissue.

"How long was I out?" I asked Jenny again.

"I don't know," she said still leaning to see around the traffic. "Nine, maybe ten hours." She turned toward me. "Why?"

I covered my arm back up and then looked straight ahead. "No reason."

Jenny started to say something else, but then stopped when the Volvo in front of us moved. "Finally," she huffed.

While the line advanced slowly, creeping down Main Street, I searched through the crowds on the sidewalk for Bill, maybe I could catch him walking by, maybe catch him leaving a store. But as we came to the end of the shops, it was all for naught.

Just before the bridge, the traffic stopped again and a man in a bright orange vest waved a tow truck, its lights flashing, from the grassy banks and onto the road. And as it turned to cross the bridge, my stomach lurched when I saw that Bill Dickerson's truck was its haul. The dark water seeped from the door seals, leaving a disturbing trail.

"Was that Bill's truck?" Jenny said, her mouth hanging open.

"Get me back to Hazel's," I said as fear of what I would find took over.

Cars lined each side of Bear Paw Lane and when we passed in front of the yellow house, I grabbed Jenny's arm. "Stop," I said, "I need to get out. Can you just find a parking spot and meet me inside?"

"Fine," she said.

I raced up the drive and into the garage, sliding to a stop when Mark stood there with Sheriff Reed and Deputy Watson. Mark and Deputy Watson turned and were taken back by my appearance, while Sheriff Reed barely blinked.

"Where's Hazel?" I said, hating the quiver in my voice.

"She's inside," Mark said, then put his hand out to stop me. "What happened to you?" he asked. "And where's our car?"

"I'm fine," I lied, then motioned toward the street. "And Jenny's parking your car right now."

It took all I had to calm my breath as I dared a glance at Sheriff Reed, thinking for a moment, he might take me into custody or tell Mark about all the damage to the Mini, anything to keep me from reaching Hazel. But instead, he just remained still and silent, and I pushed into the house.

Inside, it looked like Hazel and Mark had won some sort of Pepto-Bismol home makeover, as pink candles lined the mantle, chasing away the welcoming scent of vanilla and replacing it with one that smelled like an old lady's perfume. Pink confetti that read "It's a girl!" littered the entryway table, pink hand soap and hand towels were in the small guest bathroom near the stairs, and pink balloons, tied throughout the house, gave splashes of pink to every corner.

I squeezed my way through droves of baby-crazed women gathered in the living room and kitchen, searching fruitlessly for Hazel. But just as I started to make another round, Kiki looked up from pouring pink punch into little pink cups, and glared. "You RSVP'd," she practically growled.

"And I'm here, aren't I?"

She eyed me over, then set a cup at the end of a neat row next to a tray full of diaper-shaped cookies with pink icing. "You're a mess. You look like you just came from a bar fight," she said, exasperated. "Do you even care about your sister?"

"I already told you," I said through gritted teeth, "I'm here. Now tell me where Hazel is."

"She's upstairs still getting ready," she said.

In a breath, Kiki's foul demeanor shifted to excitement when a knock came from the front door. She pushed past me and wiped her hands on a dishtowel, then smoothed down the front of her black and white striped dress, taking a deep breath as if she was about to step out on stage to perform.

Just as Kiki opened the door to a woman with short brown hair in a flowery dress, I bounded upstairs, finding Hazel in Anna's room, looking out the window at the back lawn.

"What are you doing?" I asked, startling her. "Are you okay?"

When she turned, her eyes widened. "What happened

to you?"

"Don't worry about me. I'm fine," I said, stepping closer, checking the shadows. "What about you? How're you feeling?"

"I feel fine," she said as her belly rose beneath her pink dress. She turned back to the window, and for a moment, I wondered if Kiki had made her wear that color to match everything at the party. Probably.

I took another step toward her as I got more and more nervous. "You're party started."

Hazel didn't move.

"Did you hear me?" I asked, taking another step. "Everyone's downstairs."

This time, Hazel let out a long-suffering sigh, still gazing out the window and said, "Everyone?"

"I'm pretty sure," I said. "I think I saw Mark's mom and his two sisters in the kitchen. I wasn't introduced or anything, but they seem to have the same nose as Mark."

Hazel remained where she was.

"Oh," I added, trying to sound bright, "and a couple of your neighbors are here too. That lady with the Chihuahua, and that one who drives the black convertible."

More silence.

"There's also that girl from the grocery store," I said. "You know, the one with the tattoo on her neck."

Finally, Hazel turned around. But when I saw that her eyes were glistened with tears, I wished she had stayed facing the window. "I don't care about the girl from the grocery store, Scarlett. Is *she* here?"

I wanted to just lie to her and tell her that Mom had

made it, but what good would that have done? I would only be delaying the inevitable heartbreak. So instead, I lowered my gaze and gave her the answer.

"I'm sorry," I said, wondering if someone had had this same discussion with her on her wedding day as she waited for us to arrive.

"I don't know why I keep expecting her to show up," Hazel said as her chin quivered.

I choked back a lump. "Because she's our mom."

A silence lingered between us and I wasn't sure what I expected Hazel to do next. Maybe pull herself together and go join the party, ignoring our damaged relationship, tucking it beneath a quick grin as she headed downstairs. But what I wasn't expecting was for her raise her gaze to mine and ask, "Did you know about the wedding?"

"No," I said so softly that I almost didn't hear it myself.

She blinked and broke the connection, moving her attention to the empty crib. "I should have tried harder, Scarlett," she said, shaking her head. "I should have known what Mom was going to do."

I wanted to tell her that she was right. That she should have tried harder. That she should have known. That she was well aware of the kind of mother we had and that leaving me there, all alone, was the most selfish thing she could have ever done. But instead, I walked to the door.

"C'mon, everyone's waiting," I said, hating the way my voice betrayed me.

When I turned, Hazel stood behind me, her brow crinkled with sorrow. She pulled me into her arms and buried her head on my shoulder. "I'm so sorry, Scarlett," she cried. "I didn't know Mom hadn't told you."

Her body shook with the same grief I'd collected like coins over the last few years, placing a warped value on each wrong she'd done, shining up every moment she wasn't there when I needed her most. At that moment, I realized for the first time that it wasn't just our dad's eyes that connected us. We shared the same disappointment. We shared the same heartbreak. We shared the same deep need, deep desire, to have a mom that showed up - at a wedding, a baby shower, or to throw out a deadbeat who stole our money.

And despite everything wrong and wicked in this town, all the turmoil and anguish I had been through in the last few weeks, I found that I needed to be here. Hazel needed me to be here. If only for this single moment, when she thought she had no one.

Slowly, I wrapped my arms around my big sister, the sister I thought I'd lost forever, but somehow had found again, and cried with her.

We headed downstairs, the expected murmur of conversation absent. When Mark pushed through the crowd with a horrified expression on his face, I stopped on the last step with Hazel behind me.

"Look, I'll pay for the damages to the car," I said, wishing Hazel's and my reconciliation could have lasted longer than five minutes.

"What are you talking about?" Hazel said, glancing between Mark and me.

Something in the way Mark looked across the crowd

at Sheriff Reed, told me what he was about to say. And deep down, I think I already knew it.

Even still, my breath caught in my chest when Mark said, "Bill Dickerson's been killed."

From across the room, I saw Kiki cup her hand over her mouth and drop to the couch. "How could this happen?"

There was only one explanation: Riley Shelton.

COMING 2014

In the midst of darkness, Scarlett sees the truth.
Coming in 2014, the exciting sequel
to Saving Scarlett.

www.RandaGoode.com
facebook.com/AuthorRandaGoode

Made in the USA
San Bernardino, CA
02 October 2013